Memoirs of the Extraordinary Life, Works and Discoveries of Martinus Scriblerus

Alexander Pope
and John Arbuthnot

ET REMOTISSIMA PROPE

100 PAGES

100 PAGES
Published by Hesperus Press Limited
4 Rickett Street, London SW6 1RU
www.hesperuspress.com

First published 1741
First published by Hesperus Press Limited, 2002

Foreword © Peter Ackroyd, 2002

Designed and typeset by Fraser Muggeridge
Printed in the United Arab Emirates by Oriental Press

ISBN: 1-84391-001-2

CONTENTS

In 1714 Alexander Pope and Jonathan Swift established a literary club for what Pope confidently described as 'some of the greatest wits of the age'; the Scriblerus Club met in the rooms of John Arbuthnot, author and physician to Queen Anne, and its other members included John Gay and Thomas Parnell. Swift himself averred that it represented 'a friendship among men of genius'. It was a pardonable over-estimate, perhaps, since the men of genius among them were amply assisted by the men of wit. The *Memoirs*, then, is a comedy undertaken by the most brilliant and most facetious men of their time; as such, it has been unjustly neglected by those who prefer longer if less compelling works.

Their first thought had been to compose a satirical periodical, but the effort and expense of such an undertaking prompted them towards a single unsolemn treatise. It was entitled *Memoirs of the Extraordinary Life, Works and Discoveries of Martinus Scriblerus*, and remained unpublished until 1741 when it was included in the second volume of Pope's prose works; it was in fact a collaborative enterprise and a tract for the times designed, in the words of Pope himself, 'to have ridiculed all the false tastes in learning, under the character of a man of capacity enough that he had dipped in every art and science, but injudiciously in each.' The figure of Scriblerus was invented, in other words, to satirise all the idiocies of fashionable taste and contemporary scholarship.

It was an age of literary pedantry as well as of literature, and this text delivers a strong attack upon antiquarianism and fustian learning of every description. Martin's father, Cornelius, consults the instructions of Aristotle before having intercourse with his wife, for example, so that the birth of

Scriblerus himself can be seen as an example of misdirected pedantry. Cornelius Scriblerus, a figure based upon a noted and notorious scientist of the time, wishes to use an antique shield as a cradle for his newborn son, but falls into a faint when he discovers that his maid has scoured off all its rust. Here the authors are assaulting the connoisseurs or virtuosi of their period who loved nothing unless it were soiled with the detritus of age.

The child is born at the junction of the Seven Dials in St Giles, a notoriously dissolute area which was also well known as the home of quack astrologers; the *Memoirs* is as much an anatomy of London as of learning. His mother dreams that she has given birth to a 'huge inkhorn', accurately prophesying the activities of the adult Martin. One of the works published under his name was *Peri bathous* or *The Art of Sinking in Poetry*; this comic treatise, an attack upon poetic excess and the false sublime, was in fact a production of Alexander Pope who wished to satirise certain contemporary versifiers.

It is also a satire upon those who seek the wisdom of books rather than of experience, and so it becomes a spirited parody of all false or vain learning; in this it resembles such successful books of the period as Swift's *A Tale of a Tub* and Sterne's *Tristram Shandy*. When the young Scriblerus is dressed in a 'geographical suit of clothes', with various articles from various countries, and his gingerbread is fashioned in the shape of letters of the Greek alphabet, he might have stepped out of the land of Laputa in *Gulliver's Travels*. All these books are part of the same movement of wit.

This was also a period in which there was a great battle of texts and pamphlets between the 'Ancients' and the 'Moderns' – those who revered classical learning against those who followed the new philosophy of science and experiment.

Although the Scriblerians were by no means 'Moderns', and for example took every opportunity of attacking the members of the newly created Royal Society, they were also aware of the problems of pedantry. That is why the *Memoirs* parodies over-elaborate or 'hard' words, such as 'vectitation' for transport, and the quiddities of contemporary philosophy. Vain theological speculation is also a target, summed up by the question: 'If angels pass from one extreme to another without going through a middle?'

It is in fact a parody of every intellectual fad or fashion of the period stemming from ignorance or vanity, and it is written from the perspective of what the one sensible character in the book describes as 'a due regard for whatever was useful or excellent, whether ancient or modern'. It is the call for sanity here, as measured by what was known as 'right reason', which is typical and topical. It is what Byron meant when he described Pope as 'the great moral poet of all times, of all climes, of all feelings, and of all stages of existence'. This may seem to overpraise a poet who is better known for his satire than his wisdom, but it contains an important truth.

The *Memoirs* is also very topical. The satire on free-thinkers, who denied the existence of the soul, was directed against contemporary societies; the debate upon the exact location of the soul reflects those conducted at the time by many eminent divines. It is indeed a tract for the times, and remains a document indispensable for those who wish to understand the intellectual culture of the period.

The book also offers an engaging insight into the fantasies and curiosities of eighteenth-century London, with its periodicals and coffee-houses intent upon the manners of the age; it also reproduces a tone of voice, at once learned and comic, inspired and facetious, that is an integral aspect of the city's life. It is quite unpompous, and designed to deflate pomposity of every description. A great part of this work may confidently be ascribed to Arbuthnot, but the voices of Pope and of Swift are also to be found here. In its wit and inventiveness, therefore, it is representative of the genius of its age.

— *Peter Ackroyd, 2002*

Memoirs of
Martinus Scriblerus

INTRODUCTION TO THE READER

In the reign of Queen Anne (which, notwithstanding those happy times which succeeded, every Englishman has not forgotten) thou mayst possibly, gentle reader, have seen a certain venerable person, who frequented the outside of the palace of St James's; and who, by the gravity of his deportment and habit, was generally taken for a decayed gentleman of Spain. His stature was tall, his visage long, his complexion olive, his brows were black and even, his eyes hollow yet piercing, his nose inclined to aquiline, his beard neglected and mixed with grey. All this contributed to spread a solemn melancholy over his countenance. Pythagoras was not more silent, Pyrrho more motionless, nor Zeno more austere. His wig was as black and smooth as the plumes of a raven, and hung as straight as the hair of a river-god rising from the water. His cloak so completely covered his whole person that whether or no he had any other clothes (much less any linen) under it, I shall not say; but his sword appeared a full yard behind him, and his manner of wearing it was so stiff that it seemed grown to his thigh. His whole figure was so utterly unlike anything of this world that it was not natural for any man to ask him a question without blessing himself first. Those who never saw a Jesuit took him for one, and others believed him some high priest of the Jews.

But under this macerated form was concealed a mind replete with science, burning with a zeal of benefiting his fellow-creatures, and filled with an honest conscious pride, mixed with a scorn of doing or suffering the least thing beneath the dignity of a philosopher. Accordingly he had a soul that would not let him accept of any offers of charity, at the same time that his body seemed but too much to require it.

His lodging was in a small chamber up four pair of stairs, where he regularly paid for what he had when he ate or drank, and he was often observed wholly to abstain from both. He declined speaking to anyone, except the Queen, or her First Minister, to whom he attempted to make some applications; but his real business or intentions were utterly unknown to all men. Thus much is certain, that he was obnoxious to the Queen's Ministry; who, either out of jealousy or envy, had him spirited away, and carried abroad as a dangerous person, without any regard to the known laws of the kingdom.

One day, as this gentleman was walking about dinner-time alone in the Mall, it happened that a manuscript dropped from under his cloak, which my servant picked up, and brought to me. It was written in the Latin tongue, and contained many most profound secrets, in an unusual turn of reasoning and style. The first leaf was inscribed with these words, *Codicillus, seu Liber Memorialis, Martini Scribleri*[1]. The book was of so wonderful a nature that it is incredible what a desire I conceived that moment to be acquainted with the author, who, I clearly perceived, was some great philosopher in disguise. I several times endeavoured to speak to him, which he as often industriously avoided. At length I found an opportunity (as he stood under the piazza by the dancing room in St James's) to acquaint him in the Latin tongue that his manuscript was fallen into my hands; and saying this, I presented it to him, with great encomiums on the learned author. Hereupon he took me aside, surveyed me over with a fixed attention, and opening the clasps of the parchment cover, spoke (to my great surprise) in English, as follows:

'Courteous stranger, whoever thou art, I embrace thee as my best friend; for either the stars and my art are deceitful, or the destined time is come which is to manifest Martinus

Scriblerus to the world, and thou the person chosen by Fate for this task. What thou seest in me is a body exhausted by the labours of the mind. I have found in Dame Nature not indeed an unkind, but a very coy mistress. Watchful nights, anxious days, slender meals, and endless labours must be the lot of all who pursue her, through her labyrinths and meanders.

'My first vital air I drew in this island (a soil fruitful of philosophers) but my complexion is become adust, and my body arid, by visiting lands (as the Poet has it) *alio sub sole calentes*[2]. I have, through my whole life, passed under several disguises and unknown names, to screen myself from the envy and malice which mankind express against those who are possessed of the *arcanum magnum*. But at present I am forced to take sanctuary in the British Court, to avoid the revenge of a cruel Spaniard, who has pursued me almost through the whole terraqueous globe. Being about four years ago in the city of Madrid, in quest of natural knowledge, I was informed of a lady who was marked with a pomegranate upon the inside of her right thigh, which blossomed, and, as it were, seemed to ripen in the due season. Forthwith was I possessed with an insatiable curiosity to view this wonderful phenomenon. I felt the ardour of my passion increase as the season advanced, till in the month of July I could no longer contain. I bribed her duenna, was admitted to the bath, saw her undressed, and the wonder displayed. This was soon after discovered by the husband, who finding some letters I had writ to the duenna, containing expressions of a doubtful meaning, suspected me of a crime most alien from the purity of my thoughts. Incontinently I left Madrid by the advice of friends; have been pursued, dogged, and waylaid through several nations; and even now scarce think myself secure within the sacred walls of this palace. It has been my good fortune to have seen all the

5

grand phenomena of nature, excepting an earthquake, which I waited for in Naples three years in vain; and now, by means of some British ship (whose colours no Spaniard dares approach) I impatiently expect a safe passage to Jamaica, for that benefit. To thee, my friend, whom Fate has marked for my historiographer, I leave these my commentaries, and others of my works. No more – be faithful and impartial.'

He soon after performed his promise, and left me the commentaries, giving me also further lights by many conferences; when he was unfortunately snatched away (as I before related) by the jealousy of the Queen's Ministry.

Though I was thus to my eternal grief deprived of his conversation, he for some years continued his correspondence, and communicated to me many of his projects for the benefit of mankind. He sent me some of his writings, and recommended to my care the recovery of others, straggling about the world, and assumed by other men. The last time I heard from him was on occasion of his *Strictures* on the *Dunciad*; since when, several years being elapsed, I have reason to believe this excellent person is either dead, or carried by his vehement thirst of knowledge into some remote, or perhaps undiscovered region of the world. In either case, I think it a debt no longer to be delayed to reveal what I know of this prodigy of science, and to give the history of his life, and of his extensive merits, to mankind; in which I dare promise the reader that, whenever he begins to think any one chapter dull, the style will be immediately changed in the next.

CHAPTER I

Of the parentage and family of Scriblerus,
how he was begot, what care was taken of him before
he was born, and what prodigies attended his birth

In the city of Munster in Germany, lived a grave and learned gentleman, by profession an antiquary; who, among all his invaluable curiosities, esteemed none more highly than a skin of the true Pergamenian parchment, which hung at the upper end of his hall. On this was curiously traced the ancient pedigree of the Scribleri, with all their alliances and collateral relations (among which were reckoned Albertus Magnus, Paracelsus Bombastus, and the famous Scaligers, in old time Princes of Verona) and deduced even from the times of the Elder Pliny to Cornelius Scriblerus. For such was the name of this venerable personage; whose glory it was, that by the singular virtue of the women, not one had a head of a different cast from his family.

His wife was a lady of singular beauty, whom not for that reason only he espoused, but because she was undoubted daughter either of the great Scriverius, or of Gaspar Barthius. It happened on a time, the said Gaspar made a visit to Scriverius at Haarlem; taking with him a comely lady of his acquaintance who was skilful in the Greek tongue, of whom the learned Scriverius became so enamoured as to inebriate his friend, and be familiar with his mistress. I am not ignorant of what Columesius affirms[a], that the learned Barthius was not so overtaken but he perceived it, and in revenge suffered this unfortunate gentlewoman to be drowned in the Rhine at her return. But Mrs Scriblerus (the issue of that amour) was a

a. Columesius relates this from Isaac Vossius, in his Opuscul. p. 102.

7

living proof of the falsehood of this report. Dr Cornelius was further induced to his marriage from the certain information that the aforesaid lady, the mother of his wife, was related to Cardan on the father's side, and to Aldrovandus on the mother's. Besides which, her ancestors had been professors of physic, astrology, or chemistry, in German universities, from generation to generation.

With this fair gentlewoman had our doctor lived in a comfortable union for about ten years. But this our sober and orderly pair, without any natural infirmity, and with a constant and frequent compliance to the chief duty of conjugal life, were yet unhappy, in that Heaven had not blessed them with any issue. This was the utmost grief to the good man; especially considering what exact precautions and methods he had used to procure that blessing. For he never had cohabitation with his spouse but he pondered on the rules of the ancients for the generation of children of wit. He ordered his diet according to the prescription of Galen, confining himself and his wife for almost the whole first year to goat's milk and honey[b]. It unfortunately befell her, when she was about four months gone with child, to long for somewhat which that author inveighs against as prejudicial to the understanding of the infant. This her husband thought fit to deny her, affirming it was better to be childless than to become the parent of a fool. His wife miscarried; but as the abortion proved only a female foetus, he comforted himself that, had it arrived to perfection, it would not have answered his account; his heart being wholly fixed upon the learned sex. However he disdained not to treasure up the embryo in a vial, among the curiosities of his family.

Having discovered that Galen's prescription could not

b. Galen Lib. de Cibis boni et mali succi, cap. 3.

determine the sex, he forthwith betook himself to Aristotle. Accordingly he withheld the nuptial embrace when the wind was in any point of the south[c]; this author asserting that the grossness and moisture of the southerly winds occasion the procreation of females, and not of males. But he redoubled his diligence when the wind was at west; a wind on which that great Philosopher bestowed the encomiums of Fattener of the Earth, Breath of the Elysian Fields, and other glorious eulogies. For our learned man was clearly of opinion that the *semina* out of which animals are produced are *animalcula* ready formed, and received in with the air[d].

Under these regulations, his wife, to his inexpressible joy, grew pregnant a second time; and (what was no small addition to his happiness) he just then came to the possession of a considerable estate by the death of her uncle, a wealthy Jew who resided at London. This made it necessary for him to take a journey to England; nor would the care of his posterity let him suffer his wife to remain behind him. During the voyage, he was perpetually taken up on the one hand how to employ his great riches, and on the other how to educate his child. He had already determined to set apart several annual sums for the recovery of manuscripts, the effossion of coins, the procuring of mummies; and for all those curious discoveries by which he hoped to become (as himself was wont to say) a second Peireskius. He had already chalked out all possible schemes for the improvement of a male child; yet was so far prepared for the worst that could happen, that before the nine months were expired, he had composed two treatises of education; the one he called *A Daughter's Mirror*, and the other *A Son's Monitor*.

c. Arist. Sect. 14. Prob. 5.
d. Religion of Nature, Sect. 5. Parag. 15.

This is all we can find relating to Martinus while he was in his mother's womb: excepting that he was entertained there with a consort of music once in twenty-four hours, according to the custom of the Magi; and that, on a particular day, he was observed to leap and kick exceedingly, which was on the first of April, the birthday of the great *Basilius Valentinus*[e].

The truth of this, and every preceding fact, may be depended upon, being taken literally from the *Memoirs*. But I must be so ingenuous as to own that the accounts are not so certain of the exact time and place of his birth. As to the first, he had the common frailty of old men to conceal his age; as to the second, I only remember to have heard him say that he first saw the light in St Giles's parish. But in the investigation of this point fortune hath favoured our diligence. For one day, as I was passing by the Seven Dials, I overheard a dispute concerning the place of nativity of a great astrologer, which each man alleged to have been in his own street. The circumstances of the time and the description of the person made me imagine it might be that universal genius whose life I am writing. I returned home, and having maturely considered their several arguments, which I found to be of equal weight, I quieted my curiosity with this natural conclusion that he was born in some point common to all the seven streets; which must be that on which the column is now erected. And it is with infinite pleasure that I since find my conjecture confirmed by the following passage in the codicil of Mr Neal's will:

I appoint my executors to engrave the following inscription on the column in the centre of the seven streets which I erected:

LOC. NAT. INCLUT. PHILOS. MAR. SCR.[3]

e. Ramsey's Cyrus

But Mr Neal's order was never performed, because the executors durst not administer.

Nor was the birth of this great man unattended with prodigies. He himself has often told me that, on the night before he was born, Mrs Scriblerus dreamed she was brought to bed of a huge inkhorn, out of which issued several large streams of ink, as it had been a fountain. This dream was by her husband thought to signify that the child should prove a very voluminous writer. Likewise a crab tree, that had been hitherto barren, appeared on a sudden laden with a vast quantity of crabs[f]. This sign also the old gentleman imagined to be a prognostic of the acuteness of his wit. A great swarm of wasps played round his cradle without hurting him, but were very troublesome to all in the room besides[g]. This seemed a certain presage of the effects of his satire. A dunghill was seen within the space of one night to be covered all over with mushrooms. This some interpreted to promise the infant great fertility of fancy, but no long duration to his works; but the father was of another opinion.

But what was of all most wonderful, was a thing that seemed a monstrous fowl, which just then dropped through the skylight, near his wife's apartment. It had a large body, two little disproportioned wings, a prodigious tail, but no head. As its colour was white, he took it at first sight for a swan, and was concluding his son would be a poet, but on a nearer view, he perceived it to be speckled with black, in the form of letters; and that it was indeed a paper kite which had broken its leash by the impetuosity of the wind. His back was armed with the Art Military, his belly was filled with physic, his wings were the wings of Quarles and Withers[4], the several nodes of

f. Virgil's Laurel. Donat.
g. Plato, Lucan, etc.

11

his voluminous tail were diversified with several branches of science; where the doctor beheld with great joy a knot of logic, a knot of metaphysic, a knot of casuistry, a knot of polemical divinity, and a knot of common law, with a lantern of Jacob Behmen[5].

There went a report in the family that as soon as he was born he uttered the voice of nine several animals. He cried like a calf, bleated like a sheep, chattered like a magpie, grunted like a hog, neighed like a foal, croaked like a raven, mewed like a cat, gabbled like a goose, and brayed like an ass. And the next morning he was found playing in his bed with two owls, which came down the chimney. His father greatly rejoiced at all these signs, which betokened the variety of his eloquence and the extent of his learning; but he was more particularly pleased with the last, as it nearly resembled what happened at the birth of Homer[h].

h. Vid. Eustath. in Odyss. 1. 12. ex Alex. Paphio, et Leo Allat. de patr. Hom. pag. 45.

CHAPTER II

No sooner was the cry of the infant heard but the old gentleman rushed into the room, and snatching it in his arms, examined every limb with attention. He was infinitely pleased to find that the child had the wart of Cicero, the wry neck of Alexander, knots upon his legs like Marius, and one of them shorter than the other like Agesilaus. The good Cornelius also hoped he would come to stammer like Demosthenes, in order to be as eloquent; and in time arrive at many other defects of famous men. He held the child so long that the midwife, grown out of all patience, snatched it from his arms in order to swaddle it.

'Swaddle him!' quoth he, 'far be it from me to submit to such a pernicious custom. Is not my son a man? And is not man the lord of the universe? Is it thus you use this monarch at his first arrival in his dominions, to manacle and shackle him hand and foot? Is this what you call to be free-born? If you have no regard to his natural liberty, at least have some to his natural faculties. Behold with what agility he spreadeth his toes and moveth them with as great variety as his fingers! A power which in the small circle of a year may be totally abolished by the enormous confinement of shoes and stockings. His ears (which other animals turn with great advantage towards the sonorous object) may, by the ministry of some accursed nurse, for ever lie flat and immovable. Not so the ancients, they could move them at pleasure, and accordingly are often described *arrectis auribus*[6].'

'What a devil,' quoth the midwife, 'would you have your

son move his ears like a drill?'

'Yes, fool,' said he, 'why should he not have the perfection of a drill, or of any other animal?'

Mrs Scriblerus, who lay all this while fretting at her husband's discourse, at last broke out to this purpose:

'My dear, I have had many disputes with you upon this subject before I was a month gone. We have but one child, and cannot afford to throw him away upon experiments. I'll have my boy bred up like other gentlemen, at home, and always under my own eye.'

All the gossips with one voice cried 'Ay, ay,' but Cornelius broke out in this manner:

'What, bred at home! Have I taken all this pains for a creature that is to lead the inglorious life of a cabbage, to suck the nutritious juices from the spot where he was first planted? No, to perambulate this terraqueous globe is too small a range; were it permitted, he should at least make the tour of the whole system of the sun. Let other mortals pore upon maps, and swallow the legends of lying travellers; the son of Cornelius shall make his own legs his compasses; with those he shall measure continents, islands, capes, bays, straits and isthmuses. He shall himself take the altitude of the highest mountains, from the peak of Derby to the peak of Tenerife; when he has visited the top of Taurus, Imaus, Caucasus, and the famous Ararat where Noah's Ark first moored, he may take a slight view of the snowy Riphaeans; nor would I have him neglect Athos and Olympus, renowned for poetical fictions. Those that vomit fire will deserve a more particular attention. I will therefore have him observe with great care Vesuvius, Etna, the burning mountain of Java, but chiefly Hecla, the greatest rarity in the northern regions. Then he may likewise contemplate the wonders of the mephitic cave. When he has dived into the bowels of the earth, and surveyed the works of nature underground, and instructed himself fully in the nature of volcanoes, earthquakes, thunders, tempests, and hurricanes, I hope he will bless the world with a more exact survey of the deserts of Arabia and Tartary than as yet we are able to obtain. Then will I have him cross the seven gulfs, measure the currents in the fifteen famous straits, and search for those fountains of fresh water that are at the bottom of the ocean.'

At these last words Mrs Scriblerus fell into a trembling. The description of this terrible scene made too violent an impression upon a woman in her condition, and threw her into a strong hysteric fit; which might have proved dangerous if Cornelius had not been pushed out of the room by the united force of the women.

CHAPTER III

*Showing what befell the doctor's son and his shield
on the day of the christening*[7]

The day of the christening being come, and the house filled
with gossips, the levity of whose conversation suited but ill
with the gravity of Dr Cornelius, he cast about how to pass this
day more agreeably to his character; that is to say, not without
some profitable conference, nor wholly without observance of
some ancient custom.

He remembered to have read in Theocritus that the cradle
of Hercules was a shield; and being possessed of an antique
buckler, which he held as a most inestimable relic, he determined to have the infant laid therein, and in that manner
brought into the study, to be shown to certain learned men of
his acquaintance.

The regard he had for this shield had caused him formerly
to compile a dissertation concerning it, proving from the
several properties, and particularly the colour of the rust, the
exact chronology thereof.

With this treatise, and a moderate supper, he proposed to
entertain his guests; though he had also another design: to
have their assistance in the calculation of his son's nativity.

He therefore took the buckler out of a case (in which he
always kept it, lest it might contract any modern rust) and
entrusted it to his housemaid, with orders that when the
company was come she should lay the child carefully in it,
covered with a mantle of blue satin.

The guests were no sooner seated but they entered into a
warm debate about the *triclinium* and the manner of *decubitus*[8]
of the ancients, which Cornelius broke off in this manner:

'This day, my friends, I purpose to exhibit my son before you; a child not wholly unworthy of inspection, as he is descended from a race of virtuosi. Let the physiognomists examine his features, let the chirographists behold his palm, but above all let us consult for the calculation of his nativity. To this end, as the child is not vulgar, I will not present him unto you in a vulgar manner. He shall be cradled in my ancient shield, so famous through the universities of Europe. You all know how I purchased that invaluable piece of antiquity at the great (though indeed inadequate) expense of all the plate of our family, how happily I carried it off, and how triumphantly I transported it hither, to the inexpressible grief of all Germany. Happy in every circumstance, but that it broke the heart of the great Melchior Insipidus[9]!'

Here he stopped his speech, upon sight of the maid, who entered the room with the child. He took it in his arms and proceeded:

'Behold then my child, but first behold the shield. Behold this rust – or rather let me call it this precious *aerugo* – behold this beautiful varnish of time, this venerable verdure of so many ages…'

In speaking these words, he slowly lifted up the mantle which covered it, inch by inch; but at every inch he uncovered, his cheeks grew paler, his hand trembled, his nerves failed, till on sight of the whole the tremor became universal. The shield and the infant both dropped to the ground, and he had only strength enough to cry out, 'O God! my shield, my shield!'

The truth was, the maid (extremely concerned for the reputation of her own cleanliness, and her young master's honour) had scoured it as clean as her andirons. Cornelius sunk back on a chair, the guests stood astonished, the infant squalled, the maid ran in, snatched it up again in her arms, flew into her mistress' room, and told what had happened. Downstairs in an instant hurried all the gossips, where they found the doctor in a trance. Hungary water, hartshorn, and the confused noise of shrill voices, at length awakened him; when opening his eyes, he saw the shield in the hands of the housemaid.

'O woman, woman!' he cried, and snatched it violently from her, 'was it to thy ignorance that this relic owes its ruin? Where, where is the beautiful crust that covered thee so long? Where those traces of time, and fingers as it were of antiquity? Where all those beautiful obscurities, the cause of much delightful disputation, where doubt and curiosity went hand in hand, and eternally exercised the speculations of the learned? All this the rude touch of an ignorant woman hath done away! The curious prominence at the belly of that figure, which some taking for the *cuspis* of a sword, denominated a Roman soldier; others accounting the *insignia virilia*, pronounced to be one of the *dii termini*; behold she hath cleaned it in like shameful sort, and shown to be the head of a nail. O my shield, my shield! Well may I say with Horace, *non bene relicta parmula*.'[10]

The gossips, not at all enquiring into the cause of his sorrow, only asked if the child had no hurt, and cried, 'Come, come, all is well, what has the woman done but her duty? A tight cleanly wench I warrant her; what a stir a man makes about a *basin* that an hour ago, before this labour was bestowed upon it, a country barber would not have hung at his shop door.'

'A *basin*!' cried another, 'no such matter, it is nothing but a paltry old sconce, with the nozzle broken off.'

The learned gentlemen, who till now had stood speechless,

hereupon looking narrowly on the shield, declared their assent to this latter opinion, and desired Cornelius to be comforted, assuring him it was a sconce and no other. But this, instead of comforting, threw the doctor into such a violent fit of passion that he was carried off groaning and speechless to bed; where, being quite spent, he fell into a kind of slumber.

CHAPTER IV

*Of the suction and nutrition of the great Scriblerus
in his infancy, and of the first rudiments of his learning* [11]

As soon as Cornelius awakened, he raised himself on his elbow, and casting his eye on Mrs Scriblerus, spoke as follows:

'Wisely was it said by Homer that in the cellar of Jupiter are two barrels, the one of good, the other of evil, which he never bestows on mortals separately, but constantly mingles them together. Thus at the same time hath Heaven blessed me with the birth of a son, and afflicted me with the scouring of my shield. Yet let us not repine at his dispensations, who gives and who takes away; but rather join in prayer that the rust of antiquity, which he hath been pleased to take from my shield, may be added to my son; and that so much of it as it is my purpose he shall contract in his education, may never be destroyed by any modern polishing.'

He could no longer bear the sight of the shield, but ordered it should be removed for ever from his eyes. It was not long after purchased by Dr Woodward, who, by the assistance of Mr Kemp, encrusted it with a new rust, and is the same whereof a cut hath been engraved, and exhibited to the great contentation of the learned.

Cornelius now began to regulate the suction of his child. Seldom did there pass a day without disputes between him and the mother, or the nurse, concerning the nature of aliment. The poor woman never dined but he denied her some dish or other, which he judged prejudicial to her milk. One day she had a longing desire to a piece of beef, and as she stretched her hand towards it, the old gentleman drew it away, and spoke to this effect:

'Hadst thou read the ancients, O nurse, thou wouldst prefer the welfare of the infant which thou nourishest, to the indulging of an irregular and voracious appetite. Beef, it is true, may confer a robustness on the limbs of my son, but will hebetate and clog his intellectuals.'

While he spoke this, the nurse looked upon him with much anger, and now and then cast a wishful eye upon the beef.

'Passion,' continued the doctor, still holding the dish, 'throws the mind into too violent a fermentation; it is a kind of fever of the soul or, as Horace expresses it, a short madness. Consider, woman, that this day's suction of my son may cause him to imbibe many ungovernable passions, and in a manner spoil him for the temper of a philosopher. Romulus by sucking a wolf became of a fierce and savage disposition; and were I to breed some Ottoman emperor, or founder of a military commonwealth, perhaps I might indulge thee in this carnivorous appetite.'

'What?' interrupted the nurse, 'beef spoil the understanding? That's fine indeed. How then could our parson preach as he does upon beef, and pudding too, if you go to that? Don't tell me of your ancients, had not you almost killed the poor babe with a dish of demonial black broth?'

'Lacedaemonian black broth, thou wouldst say,' replied Cornelius, 'but I cannot allow the surfeit to have been occasioned by that diet, since it was recommended by the divine Lycurgus. No, nurse, thou must certainly have eaten some meats of ill digestion the day before, and that was the real cause of his disorder. Consider, woman, the different temperaments of different nations. What makes the English phlegmatic and melancholy but beef? What renders the Welsh so hot and choleric but cheese and leeks? The French derive their levity from their soups, frogs and mushrooms. I would not let my son dine like an Italian, lest, like an Italian, he should be jealous and revengeful. The warm and solid diet of Spain may be more beneficial, as it might endue him with a profound gravity, but at the same time he might suck in with their food their intolerable vice of pride. Therefore, nurse, in short, I hold it requisite to deny you at present not only beef, but likewise whatsoever any of those nations eat.'

During this speech, the nurse remained pouting and marking her plate with the knife, nor would she touch a bit during the whole dinner. This the old gentleman observing, ordered that the child, to avoid the risk of imbibing ill humours, should be kept from her breast all that day, and be fed with butter mixed with honey, according to a prescription he had met with somewhere in Eustathius upon Homer. This indeed gave the child a great looseness, but he was not concerned at it, in the opinion that whatever harm it might do his body, would be amply recompensed by the improvements of his understanding. But from thenceforth he insisted every day upon a particular diet to be observed by the nurse; under which having been long uneasy, she at last parted from the family, on his ordering her for dinner the paps of a sow with pig; taking it as at the highest indignity, and a direct insult upon her sex and calling.

Four years of young Martin's life passed away in squabbles of this nature. Mrs Scriblerus considered it was now time to instruct him in the fundamentals of religion, and to that end took no small pains in teaching him his catechism. But Cornelius looked upon this as a tedious way of instruction, and therefore employed his head to find out more pleasing methods, the better to induce him to be fond of learning. He would frequently carry him to the puppet show of the creation of the world, where the child with exceeding delight gained a notion of the history of the Bible. His first rudiments in profane history were acquired by seeing of raree-shows, where he was brought acquainted with all the princes of Europe. In short the old gentleman so contrived it, to make everything contribute to the improvement of his knowledge, even to his very dress.

He invented for him a geographical suit of clothes, which might give him some hints of that science, and likewise some knowledge of the commerce of different nations. He had a French hat with an African feather, Holland shirts and Flanders lace, English cloth lined with Indian silk; his gloves were Italian, and his shoes were Spanish. He was made to observe this, and daily catechised thereupon, which his father was wont to call 'travelling at home'. He never gave him a fig or an orange but he obliged him to give an account from what country it came. In natural history he was much assisted by his curiosity in signposts, insomuch that he hath often confessed he owned to them the knowledge of many creatures which he never found since in any author, such as white lions, golden dragons, etc. He once thought the same of green men, but had since found them mentioned by Kircherus, and verified in the history of William of Newbury[a].

His disposition to the mathematics was discovered very early by his drawing parallel lines on his bread and butter, and intersecting them at equal angles, so as to form the whole superficies into squares[b]. But, in the midst of all these improvements, a stop was put to his learning the alphabet, nor would he let him proceed to letter D till he could truly and distinctly pronounce C in the ancient manner, at which the child unhappily boggled for near three months. He was also obliged to

a. Gul. Neubrig. Book i. Ch. 27.
b. Pascal's Life. Locke of Educ. etc.

delay his learning to write, having turned away the writing master because he knew nothing of Fabius' Waxen Tables.

Cornelius having read, and seriously weighed the methods by which the famous Montaigne was educated, and resolving in some degree to exceed them, resolved he should speak and learn nothing but the learned languages, and especially the Greek; in which he constantly ate and drank, according to Homer. But what most conduced to his easy attainment of this language was his love of gingerbread; which his father observing, caused it to be stamped with the letters of the Greek alphabet; and the child the very first day ate as far as iota. By his particular application to this language above the rest, he attained so great a proficience therein, that Gronovius ingenuously confesses he durst not confer with this child in Greek at eight years old; and at fourteen he composed a tragedy in the same language, as the Younger Pliny had done before him[c].

He learned the Oriental languages of Erpenius, who resided some time with his father for that purpose. He had so early a relish for the eastern way of writing that even at this time he composed (in imitation of it) the *Thousand and One Arabian Tales*, and also the *Persian Tales*, which have been since translated into several languages, and lately into our own with particular elegance by Mr Ambrose Philips. In this work of his childhood, he was not a little assisted by the historical traditions of his nurse.

c. Plin. Epist. Lib. 7.

CHAPTER V

A dissertation upon playthings[12]

Here follow the instructions of Cornelius Scriblerus concerning the plays and playthings to be used by his son Martin.

'Play was invented by the Lydians as a remedy against hunger. Sophocles says of Palamedes that he invented dice to serve sometimes instead of a dinner. It is therefore wisely contrived by nature that children, as they have the keenest appetites, are most addicted to plays. From the same cause, and from the unprejudiced and incorrupt simplicity of their minds, it proceeds that the plays of the ancient children are preserved more entire than any other of their customs. In this matter I would recommend to all who have any concern in my son's education that they deviate not in the least from the primitive and simple antiquity.

'To speak first of the whistle, as it is the first of all playthings; I will have it exactly to correspond with the ancient *fistula*, and accordingly to be composed *septem paribus disjuncta cicutis*.

'I heartily wish a diligent search may be made after the true *crepitaculum* or rattle of the ancients, for that (as Archytas Tarentinus was of opinion) kept the children from breaking earthenware. The china cups in these days are not at all the safer for the modern rattles; which is an evident proof how far their *crepitacula* exceeded ours.

'I would not have Martin as yet to scourge a top, till I am better informed whether the *trochus* which was recommended by Cato be really our present top, or rather the hoop which the boys drive with a stick. Neither cross and pile, nor ducks and drakes are quite so ancient as handy-dandy, though Macrobius and St Augustine take notice of the first, and Minutius Felix describes the latter; but handy-dandy is mentioned by Aristotle, Plato, and Aristophanes.

'The play which the Italians call *cinque*, and the French *mourre*, is extremely ancient; it was played at by Hymen and Cupid at the marriage of Psyche, and termed by the Latins *digitis micare*.

'Julius Pollux describes the *omilla* or chuck-farthing, though some will have our modern chuck-farthing to be nearer the *aphetinda* of the ancients. He also mentions the *basilinda*, or king-I-am; and *myinda*, or hoopers-hide.

'But the *chytindra* described by the same author is certainly not our hot-cockles; for that was by pinching and not by striking; though there are good authors who affirm the *rathapygismus* to be yet nearer the modern hot-cockles. My son Martin may use either of them indifferently, they being equally antique.

'Building of houses, and riding upon sticks have been used by children in all ages, *aedificare casas*, *equitare in arundine longa*. Yet I much doubt whether the riding upon sticks did not come into use after the age of the Centaurs.

'There is one play which shows the gravity of ancient education, called the *acinetinda*, in which children contended who could longest stand still. This we have suffered to perish entirely; and, if I might be allowed to guess, it was certainly first lost among the French.

'I will permit my son to play at *apodidiascinda*, which can be no other than our puss in a corner.

'Julius Pollux in his ninth book speaks of the *melolouthe* or the kite; but I question whether the kite of antiquity was the same with ours. And though the *ortygokopia* or quail-fighting is what is most taken notice of, they had doubtless cock-matches also, as is evident from certain ancient gems and relievos.

'In a word, let my son Martin disport himself at any game truly antique, except one, which was invented by a people among the Thracians, who hung up one of their companions in a rope, and gave him a knife to cut himself down; which if he failed in, he was suffered to hang till he was dead; and this was only reckoned a sort of joke. I am utterly against this, as barbarous and cruel.

'I cannot conclude without taking notice of the beauty of the Greek names, whose etymologies acquaint us with the nature of the sports; and how infinitely, both in sense and sound, they excel our barbarous names of plays.'

Notwithstanding the foregoing injunctions of Dr Cornelius, he yet condescended to allow the child the use of some few modern playthings, such as might prove of any benefit to his mind, by instilling an early notion of the sciences. For example, he found that marbles taught him percussion and the laws of motion; nutcrackers the use of the lever; swinging on the ends of a board, the balance; bottle screws, the vice; whirligigs the *axis* and *peritrochia*; birdcages, the pulley; and tops the centrifugal motion.

Others of his sports were further carried to improve his tender soul even in virtue and morality. We shall only instance one of the most useful and instructive, bob-cherry, which teaches at once two noble virtues, constancy and patience; the first in adhering to the pursuit of one end, the latter in bearing a disappointment.

Besides all these, he taught him, as a diversion, an odd and secret manner of stealing, according to the custom of the Lacedaemonians; wherein he succeeded so well that he practised it to the day of his death.

CHAPTER VI

*Of the gymnastics; in what exercises Martin
was educated; something concerning music,
and what sort of a man his uncle was*

Nor was Cornelius less careful in adhering to the rules of the
purest antiquity in relation to the exercises of his son. He was
stripped, powdered, and anointed, but not constantly bathed,
which occasioned many heavy complains of the laundress
about dirtying his linen. When he played at quoits, he was
allowed his breeches and stockings; because the *discoboli*
(as Cornelius well knew) were naked to the middle only. The
mother often contended for modern sports and common
customs, but this was his constant reply:

'Let a daughter be the care of her mother, but the education
of a son should be the delight of his father.'

It was about this time he heard, to his exceeding content,
that the *harpastus* of the ancients was yet in use in Cornwall,
and known there by the name of hurling. He was sensible
the common football was a very imperfect imitation of that
exercise; and thought it necessary to send Martin into the
west, to be initiated into that truly ancient and manly part of
the gymnastics. The poor boy was so unfortunate as to return
with a broken leg. This Cornelius looked upon but as a slight
ailment, and promised his mother he would instantly cure it.
He slit a green reed, and cast the knife upward, then, tying the
two parts of the reed to the disjointed place, pronounced these
words, '*Daries, daries, astataries, dissunapiter; huat, hanat,
huat, ista, pista fista, domi abo, damnaustra*[a].' But finding to

a. Plin. Hist. Nat. lib. 17. in fine. Carmen contra luxata membra, cujus verba
inserere non equidem serio ausim, quanquam a Catone prodita. Vid. Cato
de re rust. c. 160.

his no small astonishment that this had no effect, in five days he condescended to have it set by a modern surgeon.

Mrs Scriblerus, to prevent him from exposing her son to the like dangerous exercises for the future, proposed to send for a dancing master, and to have him taught the minuet and rigadoon.

'Dancing,' quoth Cornelius, 'I much approve, for Socrates said the best dancers were the best warriors; but not those species of dancing which you mention. They are certainly corruptions of the comic and satyric dance, which were utterly disliked by the sounder ancients. Martin shall learn the tragic dance only, and I will send all over Europe till I find an antiquary able to instruct him in the *saltatio pyrrhica*[13].

'Scaliger, from whom my son is lineally descended, boasts to have performed this warlike dance in the presence of the Emperor, to the great admiration of all Germany[b]. What would he say, could he look down and see one of his posterity so ignorant as not to know the least step of that noble kind of saltation?'

The poor lady was at last inured to bear all these things with a laudable patience, till one day her husband was seized with a new thought. He had met with a saying that 'spleen, garter, and girdle are the three impediments to the *cursus*[14].' Therefore Pliny (lib. xi. cap. 37.) says that such as excel in that exercise have their spleen cauterised.

'My son,' quoth Cornelius, 'runs but heavily; therefore I will have this operation performed upon him immediately. Moreover it will cure that immoderate laughter to which I perceive he is addicted. For laughter (as the same author hath

b. Scalig. Poetic 1. 1. c. 9. Hanc saltationem pyrrhicam nos saepe et diu, jussu Bonifacii patrui, coram divo Maximiliano, non sine stupore totius Germaniae, repraesentavimus. Quo tempore vox illa imperatoris, hic puer aut thoracem pro pelle aut pro cunis habuit.

it, ibid.) is caused by the bigness of the spleen.'

This design was no sooner hinted to Mrs Scriblerus but she burst into tears, wrung her hands, and instantly sent to his brother Albertus, begging him for the love of God to make haste to her husband.

Albertus was a discreet man, sober in his opinions, clear of pedantry, and knowing enough both in books and in the world to preserve a due regard for whatever was useful or excellent, whether ancient or modern. If he had not always the authority, he had at least the art, to divert Cornelius from many extravagancies. It was well he came speedily, or Martin could not have boasted the entire quota of his viscera.

'What does it signify,' quoth Albertus, 'whether my nephew excels in the *cursus* or not? Speed is often a symptom of cowardice, witness hares and deer.'

'Do not forget Achilles,' quoth Cornelius. 'I know that running has been condemned by the proud Spartans as useless in war. And yet Demosthenes could say *aner ho pheugon kai palin machesetai*; a thought which the English Hudibras has well rendered:

For he that runs may fight again,
Which he can never do that's slain.

'That's true,' quoth Albertus, 'but pray consider on the other side that animals spleened grow extremely salacious, an experiment well known in dogs[c].'

Cornelius was struck with this, and replied gravely: 'If it be so, I will defer the operation, for I will not increase the powers of my son's body at the expense of those of his mind. I am indeed disappointed in most of my projects, and fear I must sit

c. Blackmore's *Essay on Spleen*.

30

down at last contented with such methods of education as modern barbarity affords. Happy had it been for us all, had we lived in the age of Augustus! Then my son might have heard the philosophers dispute in the porticoes of the palaestra, and at the same time formed his body and his understanding.'

'It is true,' replied Albertus, 'we have no *exedra*[15] for the philosophers, adjoining to our tennis-courts; but there are alehouses where he will hear very notable argumentations: though we come not up to the ancients in the tragic dance, we excel them in the *kybistike*, or the art of tumbling. The ancients would have beaten us at quoits, but not so much at the *jaculum* or pitching the bar. The *pugilatus*[d] is in as great perfection in England as in old Rome, and the Cornish hug in the *luctus*[e] is equal to the *volutatoria* of the ancients.'

'You could not,' answered Cornelius, 'have produced a more unlucky instance of modern folly and barbarity than what you say of the *jaculum*. The Cretans wisely forbid their servants gymnastics, as well as arms[f]; and yet your modern footmen exercise themselves daily in the *jaculum* at the corner of Hyde Park, whilst their enervated Lords are lolling in their chariots (a species of vectitation seldom used amongst the ancients, except by the old men).'

'You say well,' quoth Albertus, 'and we have several other kinds of vectitation unknown to the ancients, particularly flying chariots, where the people may have the benefit of this exercise at the small expense of a farthing. But suppose (which I readily grant) that the ancients excelled us almost in everything, yet why this singularity? Your son must take up with such masters as the present age affords; we have dancing

d. Fisticuffs.
e. Wrestling.
f. Aristot. Politic. lib. 2. cap. 3.

masters, writing masters, and music masters.'

The bare mention of music threw Cornelius into a passion.

'How can you dignify,' quoth he, 'this modern fiddling with the name of music? Will any of your best oboes encounter a wolf nowadays with no other arms but their instruments, as did that ancient Piper Pythocaris? Have ever wild boars, elephants, deer, dolphins, whales or turbots, shown the least emotion at the most elaborate strains of your modern scrapers, all which have been as it were tamed and humanised by ancient musicians? Does not Aelian tell us how the Libyan mares were excited to horsing by music[g]? (Which ought in truth to be a caution to modest women against frequenting operas; and consider, brother, you are brought to this dilemma, either to give up the virtue of the ladies, or the power of your music.)

'Whence proceeds the degeneracy of our morals? Is it not from the loss of ancient music, by which (says Aristotle) they taught all the virtues? Else might we turn Newgate into a college of Dorian musicians who should teach moral virtues to those people. Whence comes it that our present diseases are so stubborn? Whence is it that I daily deplore my sciatical pains? Alas! because we have lost their true cure, by the melody of the pipe. All this was well known to the ancients, as Theophrastus assures us[h] (whence Caelius calls it *loca dolentia decantare*[i])[16] only indeed some small remains of this skill are preserved in the cure of the tarantula.

'Did not Pythagoras stop a company of drunken bullies from storming a civil house, by changing the strain of the pipe to the sober spondaeus[j]? And yet your modern musicians want

g. Aelian. Hist. Animal. lib. xi. cap. 18. and lib. xii. cap. 44.

h. Athenaeus, lib. xiv.

i. Lib. de sanit. tuenda, c. 2.

j. Quintil. lib. I. cap. 10.

art to defend their windows from common nickers[17]. It is well known that when the Lacedaemonian mob were up, they commonly sent for a Lesbian musician to appease them, and they immediately grew calm as soon as they heard Terpander sing[k]. Yet I don't believe that the Pope's whole band of music, though the best of this age, could keep his Holiness' image from being burnt on a fifth of November.'

'Nor would Terpander himself,' replied Albertus, 'at Billingsgate, nor Timotheus at Hockley-in-the-Hole have any manner of effect, nor both of 'em together bring Horneck to common civility[l].'

'That's a gross mistake,' said Cornelius very warmly, 'and to prove it so, I have here a small lyre of my own, framed, strung, and tuned after the ancient manner. I can play some fragments of Lesbian tunes, and I wish I were to try them upon the most passionate creatures alive.'

'You never had a better opportunity,' says Albertus, 'for yonder are two apple-women scolding, and just ready to uncoif one another.'

With that Cornelius, undressed as he was, jumps out into his balcony, his lyre in hand, in his slippers, with his breeches hanging down to his ankles, a stocking upon his head, and a waistcoat of murrey-coloured satin upon his body. He touched his lyre with a very unusual sort of an *harpegiatura*, nor were his hopes frustrated. The odd equipage, the uncouth instrument, the strangeness of the man and of the music drew the ears and eyes of the whole mob that were got about the two female champions, and at last of the combatants themselves.

They all approached the balcony, in as close attention as Orpheus' first audience of cattle, or that of an Italian opera

k. Suidas in Timotheo.
l. Horneck, a scurrilous scribbler who wrote a weekly paper called *The High German Doctor*.

when some favourite air is just awakened. This sudden effect of his music encouraged him mightily, and it was observed he never touched his lyre in such a truly chromatic and inharmonic manner as upon that occasion. The mob laughed, sung, jumped, danced, and used many odd gestures, all of which he judged to be caused by his various strains and modulations.

'Mark,' quoth he, 'in this, the power of the Ionian; in that, you see the effect of the Aeolian.'

But in a little time they began to grow riotous, and threw stones. Cornelius then withdrew, but with the greatest air of triumph in the world.

'Brother,' said he, 'do you observe I have mixed unawares too much of the Phrygian; I might change it to the Lydian, and soften their riotous tempers. But it is enough. Learn from this sample to speak with veneration of ancient music. If this lyre in my unskilful hands can perform such wonders, what must it not have done in those of a Timotheus or a Terpander?'

Having said this, he retired with the utmost exultation in himself, and contempt of his brother; and, it is said, behaved that night with such unusual haughtiness to his family that they all had reason to wish for some ancient Tibicen to calm his temper.

CHAPTER VII

Rhetoric, logic and metaphysics [18]

Cornelius having (as hath been said) many ways been disappointed in his attempts of improving the bodily forces of his son, thought it now high time to apply to the culture of his internal faculties. He judged it proper in the first place to instruct him in rhetoric. But herein we shall not need to give the reader any account of his wonderful progress, since it is already known to the learned world by his treatise on this subject. I mean the admirable discourse *Peri bathous,* which he wrote at this time but concealed from his father, knowing his extreme partiality for the ancients. It lay by him concealed, and perhaps forgotten among the great multiplicity of other writings, till, about the year 1727, he sent it us to be printed, with many additional examples drawn from the excellent live poets of this present age. We proceed therefore to logic and metaphysic.

The wise Cornelius was convinced that these, being polemical arts, could no more be learned alone than fencing or cudgel-playing. He thought it therefore necessary to look out for some youth of pregnant parts, to be a sort of humble companion to his son in those studies. His good fortune directed him to one of most singular endowments, whose name was Conradus Crambe, who by the father's side was related to the Crouches of Cambridge, and his mother was cousin to Mr Swan, gamester and punster of the City of London. So that from both parents he drew a natural disposition to sport himself with words, which as they are said to be the counters of wise men, and ready money of fools, Crambe had great store of cash of the latter sort. Happy

35

Martin in such a parent, and such a companion! What might not he achieve in arts and sciences!

Here I must premise a general observation, of great benefit to mankind. That there are many people who have the use only of one operation of the intellect, though like short-sighted men they can hardly discover it themselves. They can form single apprehensions, but have neither of the other two faculties, the *judicium* or *discursus*. Now, as it is wisely ordered that people deprived of one sense have the others in more perfection, such people will form single ideas with a great deal of vivacity; and happy were it indeed if they would confine themselves to such, without forming *judicia*, much less argumentations.

Cornelius quickly discovered that these two last operations of the intellect were very weak in Martin, and almost totally extinguished in Crambe; however, he used to say that rules of logic are spectacles to a purblind understanding, and therefore he resolved to proceed with his two pupils.

Martin's understanding was so totally immersed in sensible objects that he demanded examples from material things of the abstracted ideas of logic. As for Crambe, he contented himself with the words, and when he could but form some conceit upon them, was fully satisfied.

Thus Crambe would tell his instructor that all men were not singular, that individuality could hardly be predicated of any man, for it was commonly said that a man *is* not the same as he *was*, that madmen are *beside themselves*, and drunken men *come to themselves*; which shows that few men have that most valuable logical endowment, individuality.

Cornelius told Martin that a shoulder of mutton was an individual, which Crambe denied, for he had seen it cut into commons.

'That's true,' quoth the tutor, 'but you never saw it cut into shoulders of mutton.'

'If it could,' quoth Crambe, 'it would be the most lovely individual of the university.'

When he was told a substance was that which was subject to accidents, 'Then soldiers,' quoth Crambe, 'are the most substantial people in the world.'

Neither would he allow it to be a good definition of accident, that it could be present or absent without the destruction of the subject; since there are a great many accidents that destroy the subject, as burning does a house, and death a man. But as to that, Cornelius informed him that there was a natural death and a logical death; that though a man after his natural death was not capable of the least parish office, yet he might still keep his stall amongst the logical predicaments.

Cornelius was forced to give Martin sensible images; thus calling up the coachman he asked him what he had seen at the beargarden. The man answered he saw two men fight a prize; one was a fair man, a sergeant in the guards, the other black, a butcher; the sergeant had red breeches, the butcher blue; they fought upon a stage about four o'clock, and the sergeant wounded the butcher in the leg.

'Mark,' quoth Cornelius, 'how the fellow runs through the predicaments. Men, *substantia;* two, *quantitas*; fair and black, *qualitas*; sergeant and butcher, *relatio*; wounded the other, *actio et passio*; fighting, *situs*; stage, *ubi*; two o'clock, *quando;* blue and red breeches, *habitus*.'

At the same time he warned Martin that what he now learned as a logician, he must forget as a natural philosopher; that though he now taught them that accidents inhered in the subject, they would find in time there was no such thing; and that colour, taste, smell, heat, and cold, were not in the things, but only phantasms of our brains. He was forced to let them into this secret, for Martin could not conceive how a habit inhered in a dancing master, when he did not dance; nay, he would demand the characteristics of relations.

Crambe used to help him out by telling him a cuckold, a losing gamester, a man that had not dined, a young heir that was kept short by his father, might be all known by their countenance; that, in this last case, the paternity and filiation leave very sensible impressions in the *relatum* and *correlatum*. The greatest difficulty was when they came to the tenth predicament. Crambe affirmed that his *habitus* was more a substance than he was; for his clothes could better subsist without him than he without his clothes.

Martin supposed a universal man to be like a knight of a shire or a burgess of a corporation that represented a great many individuals. His father asked him if he could not frame the idea of a universal Lord Mayor. Martin told him that never having seen but one Lord Mayor, the idea of that Lord Mayor always returned to his mind; that he had great difficulty to abstract a Lord Mayor from his fur, gown, and gold chain; nay, that the horse he saw the Lord Mayor ride upon not a little disturbed his imagination.

On the other hand Crambe, to show himself of a more penetrating genius, swore that he could frame a conception of a Lord Mayor not only without his horse, gown, and gold chain, but even without stature, feature, colour, hands, head, feet, or any body; which he supposed was the abstract of a Lord Mayor. Cornelius told him that he was a lying rascal; that a *universale* was not the object of imagination, and that there was no such thing in reality, or *a parte rei*.

'But I can prove,' quoth Crambe, 'that there are clysters *a parte rei*, but clysters are *universales*; *ergo*. Thus I prove my minor. *Quod aptum est inesse multis* is a *universale* by definition; but every clyster before it is administered has that quality; therefore every clyster is a *universale*.'

He also found fault with the advertisements that they were not strict logical definitions. In an advertisement of a dog stolen or strayed, he said it ought to begin thus: 'An irrational animal of the *genus caninum*, etc.'

Cornelius told them that though those advertisements were not framed according to the exact rules of logical definitions, being only descriptions of things *numero differentibus*, yet they contained a faint image of the *praedicabilia*, and were highly subservient to the common purposes of life; often discovering things that were lost, both animate and inanimate.

An Italian greyhound, of a mouse colour, a white speck in the neck, lame of one leg, belongs to such a lady. Greyhound, *genus*; mouse-coloured, etc., *differentia*; lame of one leg, *accidens*; belongs to such a lady, *proprium*.

Though I'm afraid I have transgressed upon my reader's patience already, I cannot help taking notice of one thing more extraordinary than any yet mentioned; which was Crambe's *Treatise of Syllogisms*. He supposed that a philosopher's brain was like a great forest, where ideas ranged like animals of several kinds; that those ideas copulated and engendered conclusions; that when those of different species copulate, they bring forth monsters or absurdities; that the major is the male, the minor the female, which copulate by the middle term, and engender the conclusion. Hence they are called the *praemissa*, or predecessors of the conclusion; and it is properly said by the logicians *quod pariunt scientiam, opinionem*: they beget science, opinion, etc. Universal propositions are persons of quality; and therefore in logic they are said to be of the first figure. Singular propositions are private persons, and therefore placed in the third or last figure, or rank. From those principles all the rules of syllogisms naturally follow.

I. That there are only three terms, neither more nor less; for to a child there can be only one father and one mother.

II. From universal premisses there follows a universal conclusion; as if one should say that persons of quality always beget persons of quality.

III. From singular premisses follows only a singular conclusion; that is, if the parents be only private people, the issue must be so likewise.

IV. From particular propositions nothing can be concluded; because the *individua vaga* are (like whoremasters and common strumpets) barren.

V. There cannot be more in the conclusion than was in the premisses; that is, children can only inherit from their parents.

VI. The conclusion follows the weaker part; that is, children inherit the diseases of their parents.

VII. From two negatives nothing can be concluded; for from divorce or separation there can come no issue.

VIII. The medium cannot enter the conclusion; that being logical incest.

IX. A hypothetical proposition is only a contract, or a promise of marriage; from such therefore there can spring no real issue.

X. When the premisses or parents are necessarily joined (or in lawful wedlock) they beget lawful issue; but contingently joined, they beget bastards.

So much for the affirmative proposition; the negative must be deferred to another occasion.

Crambe used to value himself upon this system, from whence he said one might see the propriety of the expression, 'such a one has a barren imagination'; and how common it is for such people to adopt conclusions that are not the issue of their premises. Therefore as an absurdity is a monster, a falsity is a bastard; and a true conclusion that followeth not from the premisses, may properly be said to be adopted.

'But then what is an enthymeme?' quoth Cornelius.

'Why, an enthymeme,' replied Crambe, 'is when the major is indeed married to the minor, but the marriage kept secret.'

Metaphysics were a large field in which to exercise the weapons logic had put into their hands. Here Martin and Crambe used to engage like any prize-fighters before their father and his other learned companions of the symposiacs. And as prize-fighters will agree to lay aside a buckler or some such defensive weapon, so would Crambe promise not to use *simpliciter et secundum quid*, provided Martin would part with *materialiter et formaliter*. But it was found that without the help of the defensive armour of those distinctions, the arguments cut so deep that they fetched blood at every stroke. Their theses were picked out of Suarez, Thomas Aquinas, and other learned writers on those subjects. I shall give the reader a taste of some of them.

I. If the innate desire of the knowledge of metaphysics was the cause of the Fall of Adam; and the *arbor porphyriana* the tree of knowledge of good and evil? Affirmed.

II. If transcendental goodness could be truly predicated of the Devil? Affirmed.

III. Whether one or many be first? Or if one doth not

suppose the notion of many? Suarez.

IV. If the desire of news in mankind be *appetitus innatus* not *elicitus*? Affirmed.

V. Whether there are in human understanding potential falsities? Affirmed.

VI. Whether God loves a possible angel better than an actually existent fly? Denied.

VII. If angels pass from one extreme to another without going through the middle? Aquinas.

VIII. If angels know things more clearly in a morning? Aquinas.

IX. Whether every angel hears what one angel says to another? Denied. Aquinas.

X. If temptation be *proprium quarto modo* of the Devil? Denied. Aquinas.

XI. Whether one Devil can illuminate another? Aquin.

XII. If there would have been any females born in the state of innocence? Aquinas.

XIII. If the creation was finished in six days, because six is the most perfect number; or if six be the most perfect number because the creation was finished in six days? Aquinas.

There were several others of which in the course of the life of this learned person we may have occasion to treat, and one particularly that remains undecided to this day; it was taken from the learned Suarez.

XIV. *An praeter esse reale actualis essentiae sit aliud esse necessarium quo res actualiter existat*? In English thus: whether besides the real being of actual being there be any other being necessary to cause a thing to be?

This brings into my mind a project to banish metaphysics out of Spain, which it was supposed might be effectuated by this method: that nobody should use any compound or decompound of the substantial verbs but as they are read in the common conjugations; for everybody will allow that if you debar a metaphysician from *ens*, *essentia*, *entitas*, *subsistentia*, etc. there is an end of him.

Crambe regretted extremely that substantial forms, a race of harmless beings which had lasted for many years, and afforded a comfortable subsistence to many poor philosophers, should be now hunted down like so many wolves, without the possibility of a retreat. He considered that it had gone much harder with them than with essences, which had retired from the schools into the apothecaries' shops, where some of them had been advanced into the degree of quintessences. He thought there should be a retreat for poor substantial forms, amongst the gentlemen ushers at court; and that there were indeed substantial forms, such as forms of prayer, and forms of government, without which the things themselves could never long subsist. He also used to wonder that there was not a reward for such as could find out a fourth figure in logic, as well as for those who should discover the longitude.

CHAPTER VIII

Anatomy[19]

Cornelius, it is certain, had a most superstitious veneration for the ancients; and if they contradicted each other, his reason was so pliant and ductile that he was always of the opinion of the last he read. But he reckoned it a point of honour never to be vanquished in a dispute; from which quality he acquired the title of the invincible doctor.

While the professor of anatomy was demonstrating to his son the several kinds of intestines, Cornelius affirmed that there were only two, the *colon* and the *aichos*, according to Hippocrates, who it was impossible could ever be mistaken. It was in vain to assure him this error proceeded from want of accuracy in dividing the whole canal of the guts.

'Say what you please,' he replied, 'this is both mine and Hippocrates' opinion.'

'You may with equal reason,' answered the professor, 'affirm that a man's liver hath five lobes, and deny the circulation of the blood.'

'Ocular demonstration' said Cornelius, 'seems to be on your side, yet I shall not give it up. Show me any viscus of a human body, and I will bring you a monster that differs from the common rule in the structure of it. If nature shows such variety in the same age, why may she not have extended it further in several ages? Produce me a man now of the age of an antediluvian, of the strength of Samson, or the size of the giants. If in the whole, why may it not in parts of the body be possible the present generation of men may differ from the ancients? The moderns have perhaps lengthened the channel of the guts by gluttony, and diminished the liver by hard drinking. Though it shall be demonstrated that modern blood circulates, yet I will still believe, with Hippocrates, that the blood of the ancients had a flux and reflux from the heart, like a tide. Consider how luxury hath introduced new diseases, and with them not improbably altered the whole course of the fluids. Consider how the current of mighty rivers, nay the very channels of the ocean are changed from what they were in ancient days; and can we be so vain to imagine that the microcosm of the human body alone is exempted from the fate of all things? I question not but plausible conjectures may be made even as to the time when the blood first began to circulate.'

Such disputes as these frequently perplexed the professor to that degree that he would now and then in a passion leave him in the middle of a lecture, as he did at this time.

There unfortunately happened soon after an unusual accident, which retarded the prosecution of the studies of Martin. Having purchased the body of a malefactor, he hired a room for its dissection, near the Pest-fields in St Giles's, at a little distance from Tyburn Road. Crambe (to whose care this body was committed) carried it thither about twelve o'clock at night in a hackney coach, few housekeepers being very willing to let their lodgings to such kind of operators.

As he was softly stalking upstairs in the dark, with the dead man in his arms, his burden had like to have slipped from him, which he (to save from falling) grasped so hard about the belly that it forced the wind through the anus, with a noise exactly like the crepitus of a living man. Crambe (who did not comprehend how this part of the animal economy could remain in a dead man) was so terrified that he threw down the body, ran up to his master, and had scarce breath to tell him what had happened.

Martin with all his philosophy could not prevail upon him to return to his post. 'You may say what you please,' quoth Crambe, 'no man alive ever broke wind more naturally; nay, he seemed to be mightily relieved by it.'

The rolling of the corpse downstairs made such a noise that it awakened the whole house. The maid shrieked; the landlady cried out, 'Thieves!'; but the landlord, in his shirt as he was, taking a candle in one hand, and a drawn sword in the other, ventured out of the room. The maid with only a single petticoat ran upstairs, but spurning at the dead body, fell upon it in a swoon.

Now the landlord stood still and listened, then he looked behind him, and ventured down in this manner one stair after another, till he came where lay his maid, as dead, upon another corpse unknown. The wife ran into the street and cried out, 'Murder!' The watch ran in, while Martin and Crambe, hearing all this uproar, were coming downstairs. The watch imagined they were making their escape, seized them immediately, and carried them to a neighbouring Justice; where, upon searching them, several kind of knives and dreadful weapons were found upon them. The Justice first examined Crambe.

'What is your name?' says the Justice.

'I have acquired,' quoth Crambe, 'no great name as yet; they call me Crambe or Crambo, no matter which, as to myself; though it may be some dispute to posterity.'

'What is yours and your master's profession?'

'It is our business to imbrue our hands in blood; we cut off the heads, and pull out the hearts of those that never injured us; we rip up big-bellied women, and tear children limb from limb.'

Martin endeavoured to interrupt him; but the Justice,

being strangely astonished with the frankness of Crambe's confession, ordered him to proceed; upon which he made the following speech:

'May it please your worship, as touching the body of this man I can answer each head that my accusers allege against me to a hair. They have hitherto talked like numskulls without brains; but if your worship will not only give ear, but regard me with a favourable eye, I will not be browbeaten by the supercilious looks of my adversaries, who now stand cheek by jowl by your worship. I will prove to their faces that their foul mouths have not opened their lips without a falsity; though they have shown their teeth as if they would bite off my nose.

'Now, sir, that I may fairly slip my neck out of the collar, I beg this matter may not be slightly skinned over. Though I have no man here to back me, I will unbosom myself, since truth is on my side, and shall give them their bellies full, though they think they have me upon the hip. Whereas they say I came into their lodgings, with arms, and murdered this man without their privity, I declare I had not the least finger in it; and since I am to stand upon my own legs, nothing of this matter shall be left till I set it upon a right foot. In the vein I am in, I cannot for my heart's blood and guts bear this usage. I shall not spare my lungs to defend my good name. I was ever reckoned a good liver; and I think I have the bowels of compassion. I ask but justice, and from the crown of my head to the sole of my foot I shall ever acknowledge myself your worship's humble servant.'

The Justice stared, the landlord and landlady lifted up their eyes, and Martin fretted, while Crambe talked in this rambling incoherent manner; till at length Martin begged to be heard. It was with great difficulty that the Justice was convinced, till they sent for the finisher of human laws, of whom the corpse had been purchased; who, looking near the left ear, knew his own work, and gave oath accordingly.

No sooner was Martin got home, but he fell into a passion at Crambe.

'What demon,' he cried, 'hath possessed thee, that thou wilt never forsake that impertinent custom of punning? Neither my counsel nor my example have thus misled thee; thou governest thyself by most erroneous maxims.'

'Far from it,' answers Crambe, 'my life is as orderly as my dictionary, for by my dictionary I order my life. I have made a calendar of radical words for all the seasons, months, and days of the year. Every day I am under the dominion of a certain word, but this day in particular I cannot be misled, for I am governed by one that rules all sexes, ages, conditions, nay all animals rational and irrational. Who is not governed by the word *led*? Our noblemen and drunkards are pimp-led, physicians and pulses fee-led, their patients and oranges pil-led, a new-married man and an ass are bride-led, an old-married man and a packhorse sad-led; cats and dice rat-led, swine and nobility are sty-led, a coquette and a tinderbox are spark-led, a lover and a blunderer are grove-led. And that I may not be tedious…'

'Which thou art,' replied Martin, stamping with his foot, 'which thou art, I say, beyond all human toleration – such an unnatural, unaccountable, uncoherent, unintelligible, unprofitable…'

'There it is now,' interrupted Crambe, 'this is your day for *uns*.'

Martin could bear no longer. However, composing his countenance, 'Come hither,' he cried, 'there are five pounds, seventeen shillings and nine pence: thou hast been with me eight months, three weeks, two days, and four hours.'

Poor Crambe upon the receipt of his salary fell into tears, flung the money upon the ground, and burst forth in these words: 'O Cicero, Cicero! If to pun be a crime, it is a crime I have learned from thee. O Bias, Bias! If to pun be a crime, by thy example was I biased.'

Whereupon Martin (considering that one of the greatest of orators, and even a sage of Greece had punned) hesitated, relented, and reinstated Crambe in his service.

CHAPTER IX

How Martin became a great critic

It was a most peculiar talent in Martinus to convert every trifle into a serious thing, either in the way of life, or in learning. This can no way be better exemplified than in the effect which the puns of Crambe had on the mind and studies of Martinus. He conceived that somewhat of a like talent to this of Crambe, of assembling parallel sounds, either syllables, or words, might conduce to the emendation and correction of ancient authors if applied to their works with the same diligence and the same liberty. He resolved to try first upon Virgil, Horace, and Terence; concluding that if the most correct authors could be so served with any reputation to the critic, the amendment and alteration of all the rest would easily follow; whereby a new, a vast, nay boundless field of glory would be opened to the true and absolute critic.

This specimen on Virgil he has given us, in the *Addenda* to his *Notes* on the *Dunciad*. His Terence and Horace are in everybody's hands, under the names of Richard Bentley and Francis Hare[20]. And we have convincing proofs that the late edition of Milton published in the name of the former of these was in truth the work of no other than our Scriblerus.

CHAPTER X

*Of Martinus' uncommon practice of physic,
and how he applied himself to the diseases of the mind*

But it is high time to return to the history of the progress of
Martinus in the studies of physic, and to enumerate some
at least of the many discoveries and experiments he made
therein.

One of the first was his method of investigating latent
distempers by the sagacious quality of setting-dogs and point-
ers. The success and the adventures that befell him when he
walked with these animals, to smell them out in the parks and
public places about London, are what we would willingly
relate; but that his own account, together with a list of those
gentlemen and ladies at whom they made a full set, will be
published in time convenient. There will also be added the
representation which on occasion of one distemper which was
become almost epidemical he thought himself obliged to lay
before both Houses of Parliament, entitled *A Proposal for a
General Flux*[21], to exterminate at one blow the pox out of this
kingdom.

He next proceeded to an enquiry into the nature and tokens
of virginity, according of the Jewish doctrines, which occasioned that most curious *Treatise of the Purification of Queen
Esther*[a], with a display of her case at large, speedily also to be
published.

But being weary of all practice on fetid bodies, from a
certain niceness of constitution (especially when he attended
Dr Woodward through a twelve-months' course of vomition)
he determined to leave it off entirely, and to apply himself only

a. Vid. Esther, chap. ii. v. 12.

to diseases of the mind. He attempted to find out specifics for all the passions; and, as other physicians throw their patients into sweats, vomits, purgations, etc., he cast them into love, hatred, hope, fear, joy, grief, etc. And indeed the great irregularity of the passions in the English nation was the chief motive that induced him to apply his whole studies, while he continued among us, to the diseases of the mind.

To this purpose he directed, in the first place, his late acquired skill in anatomy. He considered virtues and vices as certain habits which proceed from the natural formation and structure of particular parts of the body. A bird flies because it has wings; a duck swims because it is web-footed; and there can be no question but the aduncity of the pounces and beaks of the hawks, as well as the length of the fangs, the sharpness of the teeth, and the strength of the crural and masseter muscles in lions and tigers, are the cause of the great and habitual immorality of those animals.

First, he observed that the soul and body mutually operate upon each other, and therefore, if you deprive the mind of the outward instruments whereby she usually expresseth that passion, you will in time abate the passion itself; in like manner as castration abates lust.

Secondly, that the soul in mankind expresseth every passion by the motion of some particular muscles.

Thirdly, that all muscles grow stronger and thicker by being much used; therefore the habitual passions may be discerned in particular persons by the strength and bigness of the muscles used in the expression of that passion.

Fourthly, that a muscle may be strengthened or weakened by weakening or strengthening the force of its antagonist.

These things premised, he took notice that complaisance, humility, assent, approbation and civility were expressed by nodding the head and bowing the body forward; on the contrary, dissent, dislike, refusal, pride and arrogance were marked by tossing the head and bending the body backwards; which two passions of assent and dissent the Latins rightly expressed by the words *adnuere* and *abnuere*. Now he observed that complaisant and civil people had the flexors of the head very strong; but in the proud and insolent there was a great overbalance of strength in the extensors of the neck and muscles of the back, from whence they perform with great facility the motion of tossing, but with great difficulty that of bowing, and therefore have justly acquired the title of stiff-necked.

In order to reduce such persons to a just balance, he judged that the pair of muscles called *recti interni*, the mastoidal, with other flexors of the head, neck and body must be strengthened; their antagonists, the *splenii complexi*, and the extensors of the spine, weakened: for which purpose nature herself seems to have directed mankind to correct this muscular immorality by tying such fellows neck and heels.

Contrary to this is the pernicious custom of mothers, who abolish the natural signature of modesty in their daughters by teaching them tossing and bridling, rather than the bashful posture of stooping and hanging down the head. Martinus charged all husbands to take notice of the posture of the head of such as they courted to matrimony, as that upon which their future happiness did much depend.

Flatterers, who have the flexor muscles so strong that they are always bowing and cringing, he supposed might in some measure be corrected by being tied down upon a tree by the back, like the children of the Indians; which doctrine was strongly confirmed by his observing the strength of the *levatores scapulae*: these muscles are called the muscles of patience, because in that affection of mind people shrug and raise up the shoulders to the tip of the ear. These muscles also he observed to be exceedingly strong and large in henpecked husbands, in Italians and in English Ministers.

In pursuance of his theory, he supposed the constrictors of the eyelids must be strengthened in the supercilious, the abductors in drunkards and contemplative men, who have the same steady and grave motion of the eye. That the *buccinatores* or blowers-up of the cheeks, and the dilators of the nose, were too strong in choleric people; and therefore Nature here again directed us to a remedy, which was to correct such extraordinary dilatation by pulling by the nose.

The rolling amorous eye, in the passion of love, might be corrected by frequently looking through glasses. Impertinent fellows that jump upon tables, and cut capers, might be cured by relaxing medicines applied to the calves of the legs, which in such people are too strong.

But there were two cases which he reckoned extremely difficult. First, affectation, in which there were so many muscles of the bum, thighs, belly, neck, back, and the whole body, all in a false tone, that it required an impracticable multiplicity of applications.

The second case was immoderate laughter. When any of that risible species were brought to the doctor, and when he considered what an infinity of muscles these laughing rascals threw into a convulsive motion at the same time; whether we regard the spasms of the diaphragm and all the muscles of respiration, the horrible *rictus* of the mouth, the distortion of the lower jaw, the crisping of the nose, twinkling of the eyes, or spherical convexity of the cheeks, with the tremulous succussion of the whole human body; when he considered, I say, all this, he used to cry out, *casus plane deplorabilis!*[22] And give such patients over.

CHAPTER XI

The case of a young nobleman at court, with the doctor's prescription for the same

An eminent instance of Martinus' sagacity in discovering the distempers of the mind appeared in the case of a young nobleman at court, who was observed to grow extremely affected in his speech and whimsical in all his behaviour. He began to ask odd questions, talk in verse to himself, shut himself up from his friends and be accessible to none but flatterers, poets and pickpockets; till his relations and old acquaintances judged him to be so far gone as to be a fit patient for the doctor. As soon as he had heard and examined all the symptoms, he pronounced his distemper to be love.

His friends assured him that they had with great care observed all his motions, and were perfectly satisfied there was no woman in the case. Scriblerus was as positive that he was desperately in love with some person or other.

'How can that be,' said his aunt, who came to ask the advice, 'when he converses almost with none but himself?'

'Say you so?' he replied, 'why then he is in love with himself, one of the most common cases in the world. I am astonished people do not enough attend this disease, which has the same causes and symptoms, and admits of the same cure, with the other: especially since here the case of the patient is the more helpless and deplorable of the two, as this unfortunate passion is more blind that the other. There are people who discover from their very youth a most amorous inclination to themselves; which is unhappily nursed by such mothers as, with their good will, would never suffer their children to be crossed in love. Ease, luxury and idleness blow up this flame as well as the other. Constant opportunities of conversation with the person beloved (the greatest of incentives) are here impossible to be prevented. Bawds and pimps in the other love will be perpetually doing kind offices, speaking a good word for the party, and carry about billet-doux. Therefore I ask you, madam, if this gentleman has not been much frequented by flatterers, and a sort of people who bring him dedications and verses?'

'O Lord, sir!' quoth the aunt, 'the house is haunted with them.'

'There it is,' replied Scriblerus. 'Those are the bawds and pimps that go between a man and himself. Are there no civil ladies that tell him he dresses well, has a gentlemanly air, and the like?'

'Why truly, sir, my nephew is not awkward...'

'Look you, madam, this is a misfortune to him. In former days this sort of lovers were happy in one respect, that they never had any rivals, but of late they have all the ladies so – be pleased to answer a few questions more. Whom does he generally talk of?'

'Himself,' quoth the aunt.

'Whose wit and breeding does he most commend?'

'His own,' quoth the aunt.

'Whom does he write letters to?'

'Himself.'

'Whom does he dream of?'

'All the dreams I ever heard were of himself.'

'Whom is he ogling yonder?'

'Himself in his looking-glass.'

'Why does he throw back his head in that languishing posture?'

'Only to be blessed with a smile of himself as he passes by.'

'Does he ever steal a kiss from himself by biting his lips?'

'Oh, continually, till they are perfect vermilion.'

'Have you observed him to use familiarities with anybody?'

'With none but himself: he often embraces himself with folded arms, he claps his hand often upon his hip, nay sometimes thrusts it into – his breast.'

'Madam', said the doctor, 'all these are strong symptoms, but there remain a few more. Has this amorous gentleman presented himself with any love toys, such as gold snuffboxes, repeating watches, or tweezer-cases? Those are things that in time will soften the most obdurate heart.'

'Not only so,' said the aunt, 'but he bought the other day a very fine brilliant diamond ring for his own wearing.'

'Nay, if he has accepted of this ring, the intrigue is very forward indeed, and it is high time for friends to interpose. Pray, madam, a word or two more – is he jealous that his acquaintances do not behave themselves with respect enough? Will he bear jokes and innocent freedoms?'

'By no means; a familiar appellation makes him angry; if you shake him a little roughly by the hand, he is in a rage; but if you chuck him under the chin, he will return you a box on the ear.'

'Then the case is plain. He has the true pathognomic sign of love: jealousy; for nobody will suffer his mistress to be treated at that rate. Madam, upon the whole this case is extremely dangerous. There are some people who are far gone in this passion of self-love, but then they keep a very secret intrigue with themselves, and hide it from all the world besides. But this patient has not the least care of the reputation of his beloved, he is downright scandalous in his behaviour with himself; he is enchanted, bewitched, and almost past cure. However, let the following methods be tried upon him.

'First, let him… Secondly, let him wear a bob-wig. Thirdly,

shun the company of flatterers, nay of ceremonious people, and of all Frenchmen in general. It would not be amiss if he travelled over England in a stagecoach and made the tour of Holland in a track-boat. Let him return the snuffboxes, tweezer-cases (and particularly the diamond ring) which he has received from himself. Let some knowing friend represent to him the many vile qualities of this mistress of his. Let him be shown that her extravagance, pride and prodigality will infallibly bring him to a morsel of bread. Let it be proved that he has been false to himself, and if treachery is not a sufficient cause to discard a mistress, what is? In short, let him be made to see that no mortal besides himself either loves or can suffer this creature. Let all looking-glasses, polished toys, and even clean plates be removed from him, for fear of bringing back the admired object. Let him be taught to put off all those tender airs, affected smiles, languishing looks, wanton tosses of the head, coy motions of the body, that mincing gait, soft tone of voice, and all that enchanting woman-like behaviour that has made him the charm of his own eyes, and the object of his own adoration. Let him surprise the beauty he adores at a disadvantage; survey himself naked, divested of artificial charms, and he will find himself a forked straddling animal, with bandy legs, a short neck, a dun hide, and a pot belly. It would be yet better if he took a strong purge once a week, in order to contemplate himself in that condition; at which time it will be convenient to make use of the letters, dedications, etc. abovesaid. Something like this has been observed by Lucretius and others to be a powerful remedy in the case of women. If all this will not do, I must even leave the poor man to his destiny. Let him marry himself, and when he is condemned eternally to himself, perhaps he may run to the next pond to get rid of himself, the fate of most violent self-lovers.'

CHAPTER XII

How Martinus endeavoured to find out the seat of the soul,
and of his correspondence with the freethinkers

In this design of Martin to investigate the diseases of the mind, he thought nothing so necessary as an enquiry after the seat of the soul; in which at first he laboured under great uncertainties. Sometimes he was of opinion that it lodged in the brain, sometimes in the stomach, and sometimes in the heart. Afterwards he thought it absurd to confine that sovereign lady to one apartment, which made him infer that she shifted it according to the several functions of life. The brain was her study, the heart her state room and the stomach her kitchen. But as he saw several offices of life went on at the same time, he was forced to give up this hypothesis also.

He now conjectured it was more for the dignity of the soul to perform several operations by her little ministers, the animal spirits, from whence it was natural to conclude that she resides in different parts according to different inclinations, sexes, ages and professions. Thus in epicures he seated her in the mouth of the stomach, philosophers have her in the brain, soldiers in their hearts, women in their tongues, fiddlers in their fingers, and rope-dancers in their toes.

At length he grew fond of the *glandula pinealis*[23], dissecting many subjects to find out the different figure of this gland, from whence he might discover the cause of the different tempers in mankind. He supposed that in factious and restless-spirited people he should find it sharp and pointed, allowing no room for the soul to repose herself; that in quiet tempers it was flat, smooth and soft, affording to the soul as it were an easy cushion. He was confirmed in this by observing that calves and philosophers, tigers and statesmen, foxes and sharpers, peacocks and fops, cock sparrows and coquettes, monkeys and players, courtiers and spaniels, moles and misers, exactly resemble one another in the conformation of the pineal gland. He did not doubt likewise to find the same resemblance in highwaymen and conquerors. In order to satisfy himself in which, it was that he purchased the body of one of the first species (as hath before related) at Tyburn; hoping in time to have the happiness of one of the latter too, under his anatomical knife.

We must not omit taking notice here that these enquiries into the seat of the soul gave occasion to his first correspondence with the Society of Freethinkers, who were then in their infancy in England, and so much taken with the promising endowments of Martin that they ordered their secretary to write him the following letter:

To the learned inquisitor into Nature, Martinus Scriblerus, the Society of Freethinkers greeting.

Grecian Coffee-house, 7th May

It is with unspeakable joy we have heard of your inquisitive genius, and we think it great pity that it should not be better employed than in looking after that theological nonentity commonly called the soul. Since after all your enquiries, it will appear you have lost your labour in seeking the residence of such a chimera that never had being but in the brains of some dreaming philosophers. Is it not demonstration to a person of your sense that since you cannot find it, there is no such thing? In order to set so hopeful a genius right in this matter, we have sent you an answer to the ill-grounded sophisms of those crack-brained fellows, and likewise an easy mechanical explication of perception or thinking.

One of their chief arguments is that self-consciousness cannot inhere in any system of matter, because all matter is made up of several distinct beings, which never can make up one individual thinking being.

This is easily answered by a familiar instance: in every jack[24] there is a meat-roasting quality, which neither resides in the fly, nor in the weight, nor in any particular wheel of the jack, but is the result of the whole composition. So, in an animal, the self-consciousness is not a real quality inherent in one being (any more than meat-roasting in a jack) but the result of several modes or qualities in the same subject. As the fly, the wheels, the chain, the weight, the cords, etc. make one jack, so the several parts of the body make one animal. As perception or consciousness is said to be inherent in this animal, so is meat-roasting said to be inherent in the jack. As sensation, reasoning, volition, memory, etc. are the several modes of thinking, so roasting of beef, roasting of mutton, roasting of pullets, geese, turkeys, etc. are the several modes of meat-roasting. And as the general quality of meat-roasting, with its several modifications as to beef, mutton, pullets, etc. does not inhere in any one part of the jack, so neither does consciousness, with its several modes of sensation, intellection, volition, etc. inhere in any one, but is the result from the mechanical composition of the whole animal.

Just so, the quality or disposition in a fiddle to play tunes, with the several modifications of this tune-playing quality in playing of preludes, sarabands, jigs and gavottes, are as much real qualities in the instrument as the thought or the imagination is in the mind of the person that composes them.

The parts (say they) of an animal body are perpetually changed, and the fluids, which seem to be subject of consciousness, are in a perpetual circulation; so that the same individual particles do not remain in the brain; from whence it will follow that the idea of individual consciousness must be constantly translated from one particle of matter to another, whereby the particle A, for example, must not only be conscious, but conscious that it is the same being with the particle B that went before.

We answer, this is only a fallacy of the imagination, and is to be understood in no other sense than that maxim of the English law, that 'the King never dies'. This power of thinking, self-moving, and governing the whole machine, is communicated from every particle to its immediate successor; who, as soon as he is gone, immediately takes upon him the government, which still preserves the unity of the whole system.

They make a great noise about this individuality: how a man is conscious to himself that he is the same individual he was twenty years ago; notwithstanding the flux state of the particles of matter that compose his body. We think this is capable of a very plain answer, and may be easily illustrated by a familiar example.

Sir John Cutler had a pair of black worsted stockings, which his maid darned so often with silk that they became at last a pair of silk stockings. Now supposing those stockings of Sir John's endued with some degree of consciousness at every particular darning, they would have been sensible that they were the same individual pair of stockings both before and after the darning; and this sensation would have continued in them through all the succession of darnings; and yet, after the last of all, there was not perhaps one thread left of the first pair of stockings, but they were grown to be silk stockings, as was said before.

And whereas it is affirmed that every animal is conscious of some individual self-moving, self-determining principle, it *is answered that as in a House of Commons all things are determined by a majority, so it is in every animal system. As that which determines the House is said to be the reason of the whole assembly, it is no otherwise with thinking beings, who are determined by the greater force of several particles which, like so many unthinking members, compose one thinking system.*

And whereas it is likewise objected that punishments cannot be just that are not inflicted upon the same individual, which cannot subsist without the notion of a spiritual substance. We reply that this is no greater difficulty to conceive than that a corporation, which is likewise a flux body, may be punished for the faults and liable to the debts of their predecessors.

We proceed now to explain, by the structure of the brain, the several modes of thinking. It is well known to anatomists that the brain is a congeries of glands that separate the finer parts of the blood, called animal spirits; that a gland is nothing but a canal of a great length, variously intorted and wound up together. From the arietation and motion of the spirits in those canals proceed all the different sorts of thought. Simple ideas are produced by the motion of the spirits in one simple canal. When two of these canals disembogue themselves into one, they make what we call a proposition; and when two of these propositional channels empty themselves into a third, they form a syllogism, or a ratiocination.

Memory is performed in a distinct apartment of the brain, made up of vessels similar, and like situated to the ideal, propositional and syllogistical vessels, in the primary parts of the brain. After the same manner it is easy to explain the other modes of thinking; as also why some people think so wrong and perversely, which proceeds from the bad configuration of those glands. Some, for example, are born without the propositional or syllogistical canals; in others that reason ill, they are of unequal capacities; in dull fellows, of too great a length, whereby the motion of the spirits is retarded; in trifling geniuses weak and small; in the over-refining spirits, too much intorted and winding; and so of the rest.

We are so much persuaded of the truth of this our hypothesis that we have employed one of our members, a great virtuoso at Nuremberg, to make a sort of an hydraulic engine, in which a chemical liquor resembling blood is driven through elastic channels resembling arteries and veins by the force of an embolus *like the heart, and wrought by a pneumatic machine of the nature of the lungs, with ropes and pullies, like the nerves, tendons and muscles. And we are persuaded that this our artificial man will not only walk and speak, and perform most of the outward actions of the animal life, but (being wound up once a week) will perhaps reason as well as most of your country parsons.*

We wait with the utmost impatience for the honour of having you a member of our Society, and beg leave to assure you that we are, etc.

What return Martin made to this obliging letter we must defer to another occasion. Let it suffice at present to tell that Crambe was in a great rage at them, for stealing (as he thought) a hint from his *Theory of Syllogisms* without doing him the honour so much as to mention him. He advised his master by no means to enter into their society, unless they would give him sufficient security to bear him harmless from any thing that might happen after this present life.

CHAPTER XIV

The double mistress[25]

*NB The style of this chapter in the original memoirs is so
singularly different from the rest that it is hard to conceive by
whom it was penned. But if we consider the particular regard
which our philosopher had for it, who expressly directed that not
one word of this chapter should be altered, it will be natural to
suspect that it was written by himself, at the time when love
(ever delighting in romances) had somewhat tinctured his style;
and that the remains of his first and strongest passion gave him
a partiality to this memorial of it. Thus it begins:*

But now the successful course of the studies of Martin was
interrupted by love: love, that unnerves the vigour of the hero
and softens the severity of the philosopher. It chanced that
as Martin was walking forth to inhale the fresh breeze of
the evening, after the long and severe studies of the day,
and passing through the western confines of the famous
metropolis of Albion, not far from the proud battlements of
the palace of Whitehall, whose walls are embraced by the
silver Thames, his eyes were drawn upwards by a large square
piece of canvas, which hung forth to the view of the passing
citizens.

Upon it was portrayed by some accurate pencil the Libyan
leopard, more fierce than in his native desert; the mighty lion,
who boasted thrice the bulk of the Nemean monster; before
whom stood the little jackal, the faithful spy of the king
of beasts. Near these was placed, of two cubits high, the
black prince of Monomotapa[26]; by whose side were seen the
glaring catamountain, the quill-darting porcupine and the

man-mimicking mantiger.

Close adjoining to this, hung another piece of canvas on which was displayed the portrait of two Bohemian damsels, whom nature had as closely united as the ancient Hermaphroditus and Salmacis; and whom it was as impossible to divide as the mingled waters of the gentle Thames and the amorous Isis.

While Martin stood in a meditating posture, feasting his eyes on this picture, he heard on a sudden the sonorous notes of a clarion, which seemed of the purest crystal. In an instant the passing multitude flocked to the sound, as when a drum summons the straggling soldiers to the approaching battle. The youthful virtuoso, who was in daily pursuit of the curiosities of nature, was immediately surrounded by the gazing throng. The doors, for ever barred to the penniless populace, seemed to open themselves at his producing a silver sixpence, which (like Aeneas' golden bough) gained him admission into that scene of wonders.

He no sooner entered the first apartment but his nostrils were struck with the scent of carnage; broken bones and naked carcasses bestrewed the floor. The majestic lion roused from his bed and shook his brindled mane; the spotted leopard gnashed his angry teeth and, walking to and fro in indignation, rattled his chains.

Martin with infinite pleasure heard the history of the several monsters, which was courteously opened to him by a person of a grave and earnest mien, whose frank behaviour and ready answers discovered him to have been long conversant with different nations, and to have journeyed through distant regions. By him he was informed that the lion was hunted on the hills of Lebanon by the Pasha of Jerusalem; that the leopard was nursed in the uninhabited woods of Libya; the porcupine came from the kingdom of Prester John[27] and the mantiger was a true descendant of the celebrated Hanniman the Magnificent.

'Sir,' said Mr Randal (for that was the name of the master of the show) 'the whole world cannot match these prodigies; twice have I sailed round the globe, these feet have traversed the most remote and barbarous nations; and I can with conscience affirm that not all the deserts of the four quarters of the Earth furnish out a more complete set of animals than what are contained within these walls.'

'Friend,' answered Martin, 'bold is thy assertion, and wonderful is the knowledge of a traveller. But didst thou ever risk thyself among the Scythian cannibals, or those wild men of Abarimon, who walk with their feet backwards[a]? Hast thou ever seen the Sciapodes, so called because when laid supine they shelter themselves from the sunbeams with the shadow of their feet? Canst thou procure me a troglodyte footman, who can catch a roe at his full speed? Hast thou ever beheld those Illyrian damsels who have two sights in one eye, whose looks are poisonous to males that are adult? Hast thou ever measured the gigantic Ethiopian, whose stature is above eight cubits high, or the sesquipedalian pygmy? Hast thou ever seen any of the *cynocephali*, who have the head and voice of a dog, and whose milk is the only true specific for consumptions[b]?'

'Sir,' replied Mr Randal, 'all these have I beheld, upon my honour, and many more which are set forth in my journal. As for your dog-faced men, they are no other than what stands before you; that is naturally the fiercest, but by art the tamest mantiger in the world.'

a. Pliny, lib. 7. cap. 2.
b. Pliny, l. 16.

'That word,' replies Martin, 'is a corruption of the *mantichora* of the ancients, the most noxious animal that ever infested the Earth; who had a sting above a cubit long, and would attack a rank of armed men at once, flinging his poisonous darts several miles around him. Canst thou inform me whether the boars grunt in Macedonia? Canst thou give me a certificate that the lions in Africa are afraid of the scolding of women? Hast thou ever heard the sagacious hyena counterfeit the voice of a shepherd, imitate the vomiting of a man to draw the dogs together, and even call a shepherd by his proper name? Your crocodile is but a small one, but you ought to have brought with him the bird *trochilos*, that picks his teeth after dinner, at which the silly animal is so pleased that he gapes wide enough to give the *ichneumon*, his mortal enemy, an entrance into his belly. Your modern ostriches are dwindled to mere larks in comparison with those of the ancients; theirs were equal in stature to a man on horseback. Alas! We have lost the chaste bird *porphyrion*! The whole race was destroyed by women, because they discovered the infidelity of wives to their husbands. The *merops* too is now nowhere to be found, the only bird that flew backward by the tail. But say, canst thou inform me what dialect of the Greek is spoken by the birds of Diomedes' island? For it is from them only we can learn the true pronunciation of that ancient language.^c'

Mr Randal made no satisfactory answer to these demands, but harangued chiefly upon modern monsters and seemed willing to confine his instances to the animals of his own collection, pointing to each of them in order with his rod.

After Martin had satisfied his curiosity here, he was conducted into another apartment. Just at the entrance of the

c. Aelian, lib. 4. cap. 21; Aelian, lib. 1. cap. 2; Pliny, lib. 8. cap. 30. lib. 8. cap. 25; Pliny, lib. 11. cap. 51; Aelian, lib. 3. cap. 42; Aelian, lib. 1. cap. 49.

door appeared a Negro prince. His habiliments bespoke him royal; his head was crowned with the feather of an ostrich, his sable feet and legs were interlaced with purple and gold, spangled with the diamonds of Cornwall and the precious stones of Bristol. Though his stature was of the lowest, yet he behaved himself with such an air of grandeur as gave evident tokens of his regal birth and education. He was mounted upon the least palfrey in the universe; a palfrey whose natural beauty stood not in need of those various coloured ribbons which braided his mane and were interwoven with his tail. Again the crystal clarion sounded, and after several courteous speeches between the black prince and Martin, our youthful philosopher walked into the midst of the room, to bless his sight with the most beautiful curiosity of nature. On a sudden entered at another door the two Bohemian sisters, whose common parts of generation had so closely allied them that nature seemed here to have conspired with fortune that their lives should run in an eternal parallel.

The sun had twice eight times performed his annual course since their mother brought them into the world with double pangs. Lindamira's eyes were of a lively blue; Indamora's were black and piercing. Lindamira's cheeks might rival the blush of the morning; in Indamora the lily overcame the rose. Lindamira's tresses were of the paler gold, while the locks of Indamora were black and glossy as the plumes of a raven.

How great is the power of love in human breasts! In vain has the wise man recourse to his reason when the insinuating arrow touches his heart and the pleasing poison is diffused through his veins. But then how violent, how transporting must that passion prove, where not only the fire of youth, but the unquenchable curiosity of a philosopher, pitched upon the same object! For howsoever much our Martin was enamoured on her as a beautiful woman, he was infinitely more ravished with her as a charming monster. What wonder then if his gentle spirit, already humanised by a polite education to receive all soft impressions, and fired by the sight of those beauties so lavishly exposed to his view, should prove unable to resist at once so pleasing a passion and so amiable a phenomenon?

Martin, who felt the true emotions of love, blushed that the object of his flame should be so openly prostituted to vulgar eyes. And though he had been permitted to peruse her most secret charms, yet his honourable passion was so strong that it ran into the extreme of bashfulness; so that at the first interview he made no overtures of his love. Pensive he returned, and flinging himself on his couch, passed away the tedious hours of the night in the utmost inquietude. The rushy taper afforded a glimmering light, by which he contemplated the tender lines of Ovid; but alas! his *Remedy of Love* was no cure for our unhappy lover's anxiety! He closed the amorous volume, sighed, and casting his eyes around on the books that adorned his room, broke forth in this pathetic apostrophe:

'O ye spirits of antiquity, who yet live in those sacred leaves! Why do I make you conscious of my shame? Yet why should I depreciate the noble passion of love and call it shame? Your heroes have felt it, your poets and orators have praised it. Were I enamoured on some gaudy virgin, did I dote on vulgar perfection, the lustre of an eye, or the rose of a cheek, with reason might I blush before you, most learned inquisitors into nature! Most reverend Pliny, Aelian and Aldrovandus! Yet sure you cannot disapprove of this, which is no wanton passion, but excited by so unparalleled a production; a flame that may not only justify itself to the severity of a philosopher, but even to the avarice of a parent; since she who causes it carries a most plentiful fortune in the sole exhibition of her person. Heavens! How I wonder at the stupidity of mankind, who can affix the opprobrious name of monstrosity to what is only a variety of beauty and a profusion of generous nature! If there are charms in one face, one mouth, one body; if there are charms in two eyes, two breasts, two arms; are they not all redoubled in the object of my passion? What though she be the common gaze of the multitude and is followed about by the stupid and ignorant; does she not herein resemble the greatest princes and the greatest beauties? Only with this difference, that her admirers are more numerous, and more lasting.'

Thus sighed he away the melancholy night; but no sooner had Aurora, with blushes in her cheeks (as conscious that she was just risen from the embraces of Tithon) advanced through the purple gates of the east, but Martin rose. He rose indeed, but Melancholy, the companion of his slumbers, rose and waked with him. This was the first day that he amused himself with the gaudy ornaments of the body; that with secret pleasure he contemplated his face and the symmetry of his limbs in a looking-glass. And now forsaking his solitary apartment, he walked directly to the habitation that confined the object of his desires. But as it is observed that the curious never wander into the City to indulge their thirst of knowledge till about the hours of eleven or twelve, the morning has ever been the season of repose for all those animals who (trepanned by the frauds of men) have been obliged to change their woods and wildernesses for lodgings in cities at the rate of four shillings a week. Therefore Martin at this early hour was neither saluted by the sound of the trumpet, nor were his eyes feasted as before with the pleasing picture of his mistress; but he walked to and fro before the door with folded arms, from the hour of five to eleven, humming in a low and melancholy tune.

The trumpet no sooner sounded but his heart leapt for joy, and a second sixpence gained him a second admittance into her apartment. Yet this day also he only owned his passion in the language of his eyes. But alas! this language is only understood by those that love, and Lindamira remained still ignorant of his passion.

In the meantime it was no small cause of wonder to Mr Randal that this gentleman should come every day to behold the same show. He, no less covetous than the guardian of a rich heiress, entertained a suspicion that Martin had a design of stealing the ladies. He thereupon issued out strict orders not to admit our lover on any pretence whatsoever. What torments must this occasion in the raging fever of love?

Martin had now recourse to stratagem, and by a bribe (which often even the ermine and scarlet robe cannot resist) gained the dwarf who kept the gates of the showroom to promote his amour. He promised to convey a letter to Lindamira the same evening, if he would bring it him when darkness favoured his design, at the apartment next to the monsters. Martin, overjoyed, hastened home, and after having consulted all the authors that treat of love, composed his billet-doux, and at the time appointed went to entrust it to the hands of his confidant.

Softly he stole upstairs, approached the door and gave a gentle rap; when on a sudden a small hand was thrust through a little hole at the bottom of the door, whence issued an unintelligible squeaking voice. Martin, concluding it to be the signal, delivered his epistle, and made his retreat unobserved. He was no sooner retired but Mr Randal entered, and (as it was his usual custom before he went to bed) took a view if all were safe in the showroom. At his coming in, he saw his monkey exceedingly busy in picking the seal wax by little bits from a letter, which he turned over and over with infinite satisfaction. Mr Randal, not thinking it a breach of honour to pry into the secrets of his own family, took the letter from him and read as follows:

To the most amiable Lindamira,

While others, O darling of nature, look upon thee with the eyes of curiosity, I behold thee with those of love. Since I have been struck with thy most astonishing charms, how have I called upon nature to make a new head, new arms and a new body to sprout from this single trunk of mine, and to double every member, so to render me a proper mate for so lovely a pair! But think to how little purpose it will be for thee to stay till nature shall form another of thy kind! In such beauties she exhausts her whole art, and cannot afford to be prodigal. Ages must be numbered, nay perhaps some comet may vitrify this globe on which we tread, before we behold a Castor and a Pollux resembling the beauteous Lindamira and Indamora. Nature forms her wonders for the wise, and such a masterpiece she could design for none but a philosopher. Cease then to display those beauties to the profane vulgar, which were created to crown the desires of your passionate admirer,

Martinus Scriblerus

The dwarf entered as he was reading the letter, and perceiving his master moved with passion, immediately fell on his knees and confessed the whole affair. Mr Randal, bent on revenge, caused him to hasten to Martin's house, with assurances that Lindamira had read his letter with infinite satisfaction, and conjured him that he would immediately favour her escape.

Martin, overjoyed at the news, flew thither on the wings of love. The perfidious dwarf conducted him upstairs in the dark, gently opened the door and bid him enter. How happy was Martin in that instant, who thought of nothing but leaping into the four soft arms of his mistress! When lo – on a sudden he saw at the further end of the room two glittering balls of fire, which rolled to and fro in a most terrible manner. Immediately his ears were invaded with horrid hissings and spittings, the balls of fire drew nearer him, and the noise redoubled as he approached.

Our philosopher, bold and resolute with love, ventured towards it; when all at once he perceived something grasp him hard by the throat, and fix as it were sharp lancets in his cheek, so that blood trickled amain down his chin. Thrice Martin essayed to free himself, but vain were all his endeavours: till at length, to save his life, he was forced to betray his intrigue and alarm the house with reiterated cries of murder.

The apartment of the Bohemian beauties being the adjoining room, they were the first that entered with a light to his assistance. Martin, all bloody as he was, a most fierce catamountain hanging at his chin (which Mr Randal had maliciously placed there on purpose), at the sight of Lindamira forgot his distress.

'Ah, my love!' he cried, 'how like is thy fate to that of Thisbe, who staying but a moment too late, found, as she thought, her miserable lover torn in pieces by a savage beast!'

The affrighted damsels shrieked aloud; Mr Randal with all his retinue rushed into the room; and now every hand conspired to free his under-jaw from the sharp teeth of the enraged monster. But the lady, whose heart melted at the piteous spectacle, was so zealous in this office of humanity, that the catamountain, provoked at her good-natured diligence, leapt furiously on her and wounded three of her hands and her two noses, to such a barbarous degree that she was not fit to be shown publicly for the space of three weeks.

The generous lover, more wounded at this spectacle than by all the scratches he had himself received, charged the monster again with the utmost intrepidity and rescued his mangled mistress. Then (having taken her by the hand, and given it a gentle grasp) he retreated with his eye fixed upon her, and just as he left the room (in a low and tender accent) thus breathed forth his soul: 'Behold, all this have I suffered for you.'

Such and so modest was the first declaration of love made on this eminent occasion by our youthful philosopher. Nor was it ungently received by the simple and innocent Lindamira, who, hitherto unused to the soft protestations of adoring slaves, had rather been wondered at than beloved, and received but imperfect notions of that tender language from the addresses only of the black prince or the dwarf.

Martin, notwithstanding this unfortunate adventure, still pursued his wishes. His letters were now no more intercepted. Lindamira read them, and behaved like other courteous dames when they receive those amorous testimonials; concealed them from her guardian and returned the most engaging answers. In short, she was so far captivated as to resolve no longer to be gazed at like a public beauty in her own assembly, but retire from the world and become the virtuous mistress of a family.

But Fate had so ordained that Martin was not more enamoured on Lindamira than Indamora was on Martin. She, jealous that her sister had the greatest share in this conquest, resented that an equal application had not been made to herself. She teased Lindamira to such a degree on this subject as made her promise to see Martin no more. But then again might Indamora be deemed the unhappiest of women, whom her passion and imprudence had robbed of the sight of her lover. Yet shame caused her to conceal those anxieties from her sister. And let the reader judge how unhappy the nymph must be, who was even deprived the universal relief of a soliloquy. However, thus she thought, without being allowed to tell it to any grove or purling stream:

'Wretched Indamora! If Lindamira must never more see Martin, Martin shall never again bless the eyes of Indamora. Yet why do I say wretched, since my rival can never possess my lover without me? The pangs that others feel in absence from the thought of those joys that bless their rivals can never sting thy bosom; nor can they mortify thee by making thee a witness without giving thee at the same time a share of their endearments. Change then thy proceeding, Indamora; thy jealousy must act a new and unheard-of part, and promote the interest of thy rival as the only way to the enjoyment of thy lover.'

From that moment she studied by all methods to advance her sister's amour, and in that her own. And thus there appeared in these three lovers as extraordinary a conjunction of passions as of persons. Love had reconciled himself to his mortal foes: to philosophy in Martin and to jealousy in Indamora.

And now flourished the amour of Martin; success even prevented his wishes, the marriage was agreed on and the day appointed. Sunday was the time when Mr Randal's absence favoured their hopes, who never on that day omitted taking the fresh air in the fields. The key of the door he always took with him.

Crambe was ready laid at a convenient distance, who accommodated them with a ladder of ropes. The ladder was thrown up, and the signal given at the window. Lindamira hastened to the alarm of love, when behold a new disaster! As she was getting out of the window, the weight of her body on one side and that of Indamora's on the other, unluckily caused them to stick in the midway. Lindamira hung with her coats stripped up to the navel without, and Indamora in no less immodest posture within.

The mantiger, who for his gentleness was allowed to walk at large in the house, was so heightened at this sight, that he rushed upon Indamora like a barbarous ravisher. Indamora cried aloud for help. Martin flew to revenge this insolent attempt of a rape on his wedding day. The lustful monster, driven from our double Lucrece, fled into the middle of the room, pursued by the valorous and indignant Martin. Three times the hot mantiger, frighted at the furious menaces of his antagonist, made a circle round the chamber, and three times the swift-footed Martin pursued him.

He caught up the horn of a unicorn, which lay ready for the entertainment of the curious spectator, and brandishing it over his head in airy circles, hurled it against the hairy son of Hanniman; who, wrinkling his brown forehead and gnashing his teeth in indignation, stooped low. The horny lance just razed his left shoulder, and stuck into the tapestry hangings.

Provoked at this, the grinning offspring of Hanniman caught up the pointed horn of an antelope and aimed a blow against his undismayed adversary. Our heroic lover, who held his hat before him like a shield, received the weapon full on the crown; it pierced the beaver, and gave a small rent to his breeches. Then the human champion flung with mighty violence the hinder foot of an elk, which hit the bestial combatant full on the nether jaw. He reeled, but soon recovering, and his skill in war lying rather in the close fight that in projectile weapons, he endeavoured to close with him. Forthwith assailing him behind unawares, he clambered up his back and plucked up by the roots a mighty grasp of hair – but Martin soon dismounted him and kept him at a distance.

Love not only inspired his breast with courage, but gave double strength to his sinews; he heaved up the hand of a prodigious sea monster; which when the chattering champion beheld, he no less furious wielded the ponderous thigh bone of a giant. And now they stood opposed to each other, like the dread captain of the sevenfold shield and the redoubted Hector.

The thigh bone missed its aim; but the hand of the sea monster descended directly on the head of the sylvan ravisher. The monster chattered horrible; he stretched his quivering limbs on the floor, and eternal sleep locked fast his eyelids.

The lady from the window, like another Helen from the Trojan wall, was witness of the combat caused by her own beauty. She saw with what gracefulness her hero entered the lists, admired his activity and courage in the combat, and was a joyful witness of his triumph. She gave a spring from the window, and with open arms and legs embraced the neck and shoulders of her champion. Our philosopher received her with his face turned modestly from her, and in that manner conveyed her into the street. He called a chair with all haste, but no chairman would take her; which obliged him to bear his extraordinary burden till he found a coach, in which he carried her off, and was happily united to her that very evening, by a reverend clergyman in the Fleet[28], in the holy bands of matrimony.

CHAPTER XV

*Of the strange and never to be paralleled
process at law upon the marriage of Scriblerus,
and the pleadings of the advocates*

But Nemesis, who delights in traversing the best-laid designs of Cupid, maliciously contrived the means to make these three lovers unhappy. No sooner had the master of the show received notice of their flight but he seized on the Bohemian ladies by a warrant; and not content with having recovered the possession of them, resolved to open all the sluices of the law upon Martin. So he instantly went to counsel to advise upon all possible methods of revenge.

The first point he proceeded on was the property of his monster, and the question propounded was 'whether slaves could marry without the consent of their master'[a]. To this he was answered in the affirmative, but told at the same time 'that the marriage did not exempt them from servitude'[b].

This put him in no small hopes of having Martin added to his show, and acquiring a property in his bodily issue by the ladies. But his joy was soon dashed when he was informed that, since Martin was a free man, 'the children must follow the condition of the father, or that indeed, if they were to follow that of their mother, the case would be the same, there being no slavery in England'[c].

Then his counsel judged it more advisable to plead for a dissolution of the marriage, upon the impossibility of conjugal dues in the wife. But then the canon law allowed a triennial

a. An servi possint, invitis dominis, matrimonium contrahere?
b. An servus matrimonio eximitur a domini obsequio?
c. An liberi sequuntur conditionem patris, an matris?

cohabitation, which entirely ruined this project also. Besides, it was evident by the same law that 'monstrosity could not incapacitate from marriage,' witness the case of hermaphrodites, who are allowed *'facultatem conjugii*, provided they make election before the parish priest in what sex they will act, and take an oath never to perform in the other capacity'[d].

It was next consulted whether Martin should not be permitted to take away his wife, since, upon his so doing, 'he might be sued for a rape upon the body of her sister, there being plainly the four conditions of a rape'[e]. But then again they considered that Martin might answer he claimed nothing but his own; and if another person had fixed herself to his wife, he must not for that cause be debarred the use of his property.

Yet still, upon the same head of Martin's possessing his spouse, a suit might be devised in the name of Lindamira, on this account: that a 'wife was not obliged to live with a concubine[f], and such her sister Indamora must be accounted to Martin from the common proofs'[g]. To this too it was replied that the law ordered the wife to reside with the husband if there were sufficient security given to expel the concubine. So Martin might say he was ready to accomplish his part of the covenant if his wife would perform hers, and consent to the incision[h]. But this being an impossibility on the side of the wife, it could no way be exacted of the husband.

At length Mr Randal, being vexed to the heart, to have been so long and so quaintly disappointed, determined to commence a suit against Martin for bigamy and incest.

d. Sanchez, Hostiens. Sylvest.

e. Violentia, causa libidinis, traductio ad locum, mulier honesta.

f. Uxor non tenetur vivere cum viro concubinam tenente.

g. Tactus, amplexus, cohabitatio.

h. An uxor tenetur incisionem pati? Sanchez de Matrimonio.

Meanwhile he left no artifice or address untried to perplex the unhappy philosopher. He even contrived with infinite cunning to alienate Indamora's affections from him, and debauched her into an intrigue with a creature of his own, the black prince, whom he secretly caused to marry her while her sister was asleep.

Hereupon Martin was reduced to turn plaintiff, and commenced a suit in the spiritual court against the black prince, for cohabitation with his said wife. He was advised to insist upon a new point, viz. 'that Lindamira and Indamora together made up but one lawful wife'.

The monster-master, further to distress Martin, forced Lindamira to petition for aliment, *lite pendente*[29]: which was no sooner allowed her by the court but he obliged her to allege that 'it was not sufficient to maintain both herself and her sister; and if her sister perished, she could not live with the dead body about her'.

Martin now began to repent that he had not executed a resolution he formerly conceived of marrying Crambe to Indamora as an expedient to have made all secure. Moreover, it was insisted on, that the other also had a right to aliment, 'because, if Martin's wife should prove with child, the said sister must necessarily perform the offices of a wife, in contributing to the nutrition and gestation of the said child'.

A jury of physicians being empanelled, declared that as to nutrition they were doubtful whether any blood of Lindamira circulated through Indamora: but as to gestation, it was evidently true. And upon this, Martin was ordered to allow aliment to both, the black prince appearing insolvent.

The court proceeded to the trial. And as both the cause and the pleadings are of an extraordinary nature, we think fit here to insert them at length.

Dr Pennyfeather thus pleaded for Martinus Scriblerus the plaintiff:

'I appear before your Honour on behalf of Martinus Scriblerus, bachelor of physic, in a complaint against Ebn-Hai-Paw-Waw, commonly called the black prince of Monomotapa; inasmuch as the said Ebn-Hai-Paw-Waw hath maliciously, forcibly and unlawfully seized, ravished and detained Lindamira-Indamora, the wife of the said Martin, and the body of the said Lindamira-Indamora, from time to time ever since hath wickedly, lewdly and indecently used, handled, and evil entreated. And in order to make this his villainy more lasting, hath presumed to marry this our wife, pretending to give his wickedness the sanction of a law. And forasmuch as the adulterer doth not deny the fact, but insists upon his said marriage as lawful, we cannot open the case more plainly to your Honour than by answering his reasons, which, indeed, to mention is to confute.

'He maintains no less an absurdity than this: that one is two, and that Lindamira-Indamora, the individual wife of the plaintiff, is not one, but two persons. And that the said Ebn-Hai-Paw-Waw is not married to Lindamira, the wife of the said Martin, but to his own lawful wife Indamora, another individual person distinct from the said Lindamira, though joined to her by a strong ligament of nature.

'In answer whereunto, we shall prove three things: first, that the said Lindamira-Indamora, now our lawful wife, makes but one individual person; secondly, that if they made two individual persons, yet they constitute but one wife; thirdly, that supposing they made two individual persons and two wives, each lawfully married to her own husband, yet prince Ebn-Hai-Paw-Waw hath no right to detain Lindamira, our lawfully wedded wife, on pretence of being married to Indamora.

'As to the first point: it will be necessary to determine the constituent principle and essence of individuality, which, in respect to mankind, we take to be one simple identical soul in one simple identical body. The individuality, sameness, or identity of the body is not determined (as some vainly imagine) by one head and a certain number of arms, legs and other members, but in one simple, single *aidoion*, or member of generation.

'Let us search profane history, and we shall find Geryon with three heads, and Briareus with a hundred hands. Let us search sacred history, and we meet with one of the sons of the giants with six fingers to each hand and six toes to each foot; yet none ever accounted Geryon or Briareus more than one person. And give us leave to say, the wife of the said Geryon would have had a good action against any women who should have espoused themselves to the two other heads of that monarch. The reason is plain: because each of these having but one simple *aidoion*, or one member of generation, could be looked upon as but one single person.

'In conformity to this, when we behold this one member, we distinguish the sex and pronounce it a man or a woman, or, as the Latins express it, *unus vir, una mulier; un homme, une femme*; one man, one woman. For the same reason man and wife are said to be one flesh, because united in that part which constitutes the sameness and individuality of each sex.

'And, as where there is but one member of generation there is but one body, so there can be but one soul; because the said organ of generation is the seat of the soul; and consequently, where there is but one such organ, there can be but one soul. Let me here say, without injury to truth, that no philosopher, either of the past or present age, hath taken more pains to discover where the soul keeps her residence than the plaintiff, the learned Martinus Scriblerus. And after his most diligent enquiries and experiments, he hath been verily persuaded that the organ of generation is the true and only seat of the soul. That this part is seated in the middle, and near the centre of the whole body, is obvious to your Honour's view. From thence, like the sun in the centre of the world, the soul dispenses her warmth and vital influence. Let the brain glory in the wisdom of the aged, the science of the learned, the policy of the statesman and the invention of the witty; the accidental amusements and emanations of the soul, and mortal as the possessors of them! It is to the organs of generation that we owe man himself; there the soul is employed in works suitable to the dignity of her nature and (as we may say) sits brooding over ages yet unborn.

'We need not tell your Honour that it has been the opinion of many most learned divines and philosophers that the soul, as well as the body, is produced *ex traduce*[30]. This doctrine has been defended by arguments irrefragable, and accounts for difficulties, without it, inexplicable. All which arguments conclude with equal strength for the soul's being seated in the organs of generation. For since the whole man, both soul and body, is there formed, and since nothing can operate but where it is, it follows that the soul must reside in that individual place, where she exerts her generative and plastic[31] powers.

'This our doctrine is confirmed by all those experiments which conspire to prove the absolute dominion which that part hath over the whole body. We see how many women, who are deaf to the persuasions of the eloquent, the insinuations of the crafty and the threats of the imperious, are easily governed by some poor loggerhead, unfurnished with the least art but that of making immediate application to this seat of the soul.

The impressions made by the ear are so distant, and transmitted through so many windings, that they lose their energy. But your Honour, by immediately applying to the organ of generation, acts like a bold and wise petitioner, who goes straight to the very throne and judgement seat of the monarch.

'And whereas it is objected that here are two wills, and therefore two different persons, we answer, if multiplicity of wills implied multiplicity of persons, there are few husbands but what are guilty of polygamy, there being in the same woman great and notorious diversity of wills. A point which we shall not need to insist upon before any married person, much less of your Honour's experience.

'Thus we have made good our first and principal point: that if the wife of the plaintiff, Lindamira-Indamora, hath but one organ of generation, she is but one individual person, in the truest and most proper sense of individuality. And that the matter of fact is so, we are willing to put upon a fair trial by a jury of matrons, whom your Honour shall think fit to nominate and appoint, to inspect the body of the said Lindamira-Indamora.

'Secondly, we are to prove that though Lindamira-Indamora were two individual persons, consisting each of a soul and body, yet, if they have but one organ of generation, they can constitute but one wife. For from whence can the unity of any thing be denominated but from that which constitutes the essence or principal use of it? Thus, if a knife or hatchet have but one blade, though two handles, it will properly be denominated but one knife, or one hatchet; inasmuch as it hath but one of that which constitutes the essence or principal use of a knife or hatchet. So if there were not only one, but twenty *supposita rationalia*[32] with one common organ of generation, that one system would only make one wife. Upon the whole, let not a few heads, legs or arms extraordinary, bias your Honour's judgement and deprive the plaintiff of his legal property.

'In which right our client is so strongly fortified that, allowing both the former propositions to be false, and that there were two persons, two bodies, two rational souls, yea, and two organs of generation, yet would it still be plain in the third place, that the defendant, prince Ebn-Hai-Paw-Waw, can have no right to detain from the plaintiff his lawfully wedded wife, Lindamira. For, abstracting from the priority of the marriage of our client, by which it would seem he acquired a property in his wife and all other matter inseparable annexed unto her, it is evident prince Ebn-Hai-Paw-Waw, by his marriage to Indamora, could never acquire any property in Lindamira; nor can produce any cause why both of them should live with himself rather than with the other. Therefore, we humbly hope your Honour will order the body of our said wife to be restored to us, and due censure passed on the said Ebn-Hai-Paw-Waw.'

Dr Pennyfeather having thus ended, his pleading was thus answered by Dr Leatherhead:

'I will not trouble your Honour with any unnecessary preamble, or false colours of eloquence, which truth hath no need of, and which would prove too thin a veil for falsehood before the penetrating eyes of your Honour. In answer therefore to what our learned brother, Dr Pennyfeather, hath asserted, we shall labour to demonstrate: first, that though there were but one organ of generation, yet are there two distinct persons; secondly, that although there were but one organ of generation, so far would it be from giving the plaintiff any right to the body of Indamora, the wife of Ebn-Hai-Paw-Waw, that it will subject the plaintiff to the penalty of incest, or of bigamy; thirdly, we doubt not to prove that the said Lindamira-Indamora hath two distinct parts of generation.

'And first we will show that neither the individual essence of mankind nor the seat of the soul doth reside in the organ of generation; and this first from reason. For unreasonable indeed must it be, to make *that* the seat of the rational soul, which alone sets us on a level with beasts; or to conceive that the essence of unity and individuality should consist in that which is the source of discord and division. In a word, what can be a greater absurdity than to affirm bestiality to be the essence of humanity, darkness the centre of light, and filthiness the seat of purity?

'We could, from the authority of the most eminent philosophers of all ages, confirm this our assertion; few of whom ever had the impudence to degrade this queen, the rational soul, to the very lowest and vilest apartment, or rather sink of her whole palace. But we shall produce still a greater authority than these to manifest that personal individuality did subsist when there was no such generative carnality.

'It hath been strenuously maintained by many holy divines (and particularly by Thomas Aquinas) that our first parents, in the state of innocence, did in no wise propagate their species after the present common manner of men and beasts; but that the propagation at that time must have been by intuition, coalition of ideas, or some pure and spiritual manner, suitable to the dignity of their station. And though the sexes were distinguished in that state, yet it is plain it was not by parts such as we have at present; since, if our first parents had any such, they must have known it; and it is written that they discovered them not till after the Fall; when it is probable those parts were the immediate excrescence of sin, and only grew forth to render them fitter companions for those beasts among which they were driven.

'It is a maxim in philosophy that *generatio unius est corruptio alterius*[33]; whence it is apparent that the paradisical generation was of a different nature from ours, free from all corruption and imbecility. This is further corroborated by the authority of those doctors of the Church who have asserted that, before the Fall, Adam was endowed with a continual uninterrupted faculty of generation; which can be explained of no other than of that intuitive generation abovesaid. Since it is well known to all, even the least skilled in anatomy, that the present (male) part of generation is utterly incapable of this continual faculty.

'We come now to our second point, wherein the advocate for the plaintiff asserteth that if there were two persons and one organ of generation, this system would constitute but one wife. This will put the plaintiff still in a worse condition, and render him plainly guilty of bigamy, rape or incest. For if there be but one such organ of generation, then both the persons of Lindamira and Indamora have an equal property in it, and what is Indamora's property cannot be disposed of without her consent. We therefore bring the whole to this short issue: whether the plaintiff Martinus Scriblerus had the consent of Indamora or not. If he hath had her consent, he is guilty of bigamy; if not, he is guilty of a rape, or incest, or both.

'The defendant, prince Ebn-Hai-Paw-Waw, having been lately baptised, hath with singular modesty abstained from consummation with his said wife until he shall be satisfied from the opinion of your Honour, his learned judge, how far in law and conscience he may proceed; and therefore he cannot affirm much, nor positively, as to the structure of the organ of generation of this his wife Indamora. Yet make we no doubt that it will upon inspection appear that the said organ is distinct from that of Lindamira: whereupon we crave to hear the report of the jury of matrons, appointed to inspect the body of the said gentlewoman.

'And if the matter of fact be thus, give me your Honour's permission to repeat what hath been said by the advocate for the plaintiff; to wit, that Martinus Scriblerus, bachelor in physic, by this his marriage with Lindamira, could in no wise acquire any property in the body of Indamora, nor show any cause why this duplicated wife Lindamira-Indamora should abide with him rather than with the defendant, prince Ebn-Hai-Paw-Waw of Monomotapa.'

The jury of matrons having made their report, and it appearing from thence that the parts of generation in Lindamira and Indamora were distinct, the judge took time to deliberate, and the next court-day he spoke to this effect:

'Gentlemen, I am of opinion that Lindamira and Indamora are distinct persons, and that both the marriages are good and valid. Therefore I order you, Martinus Scriblerus, bachelor in physic, and you, Ebn-Hi-Paw-Waw, prince of Monomotapa, to cohabit with your wives, and to lie in bed, each on the side of his own wife. I hope, gentlemen, you will seriously consider that you are under a stricter tie than common brothers-in-law; that being, as it were, joint proprietors of one common tenement, you will so behave as good fellow-lodgers ought to do, and with great modesty each to his respective sister-in-law, abstaining from all further familiarities than what conjugal duties do naturally oblige you to. Consider also by how small limits the duty and the trespass is divided, lest, while ye discharge the duty of matrimony, ye heedlessly slide into the sin of adultery.'

This sentence pleased neither party; and Martin appealed

from the consistory to the Court of Arches, but they confirmed the sentence of the consistory.

It was at last brought before a commission of delegates, who, having weighed the case, reversed the sentence of the inferior courts and disannulled the marriage upon the following reasons: that allowing the manner of cohabitation enjoined to be practicable (though highly inconvenient), yet the *ius petendi et reddendi debitum conjugale* being at all times equal in both husbands and both wives, and at the same time impossible in more than one, two persons could not have a right to the entire possession of the same thing at the same time; nor could one so enjoy his property as to debar another from the use of his, who has an equal right. So much as to the *debitum petendi*; and as to the *debitum reddendi*, *nemo tenetur ad impossibile*.[34] Therefore the lords, with great wisdom, dissolved both marriages as proceeding upon a natural, as well as legal, absurdity.

CHAPTER XVI

Of the secession of Martinus and some hint of his travels [35]

This affair being thus unhappily terminated, and become
the whole talk of the town, Martinus, unable to support the
affliction, as well as to avoid the many disagreeable conse-
quences, resolved to quit the kingdom.

But we must not here neglect to mention that, during the
whole course of this process, his continual attendance on the
courts in his own cause, and his invincible curiosity for all that
passed in the causes of others, gave him a wonderful insight
into this branch of learning, which must be confessed to have
been so improved by the moderns as beyond all comparison
to exceed the ancients.

From the day his first bill was filed, he began to collect
reports; and before his suit was ended, he had time abun-
dantly sufficient to compile a very considerable volume. His
anger at his ill success caused him to destroy the greatest part
of these reports, and only to preserve such as discovered most
of the chicanery and futility of the practice. These we have
some hopes to recover, if they were only mislaid at his re-
moval; if not, the world will be enough instructed to lament
the loss by the only one now public, viz. *The Case of Straddling
and Stiles* [36], in an action concerning certain black and white
horses.

We cannot wonder that he contracted a violent aversion to
the law, as is evident from a whole chapter of his *Travels*. And
perhaps his disappointment gave him also a disinclination to
the fair sex, for whom on some occasions he does not express
all the respect and admiration possible. This doubtless must
be the reason that in no part of his *Travels* we find him beloved

by any strange princess; nor have we the least account that he ever relapsed into this passion except what is mentioned in the introduction of the Spanish lady's phenomenon.

It was in the year 1699 that Martin set out on his travels. Thou wilt certainly be very curious to know what they were. It is not yet time to inform thee. But what hints I am at liberty to give, I will.

Thou shalt know then that in his first voyage he was carried by a prosperous storm to a discovery of the remains of the ancient pygmean empire.

That in his second he was as happily shipwrecked on the land of the giants, now the most humane people in the world.

That in his third voyage he discovered a whole kingdom of philosophers who govern by the mathematics; with whose admirable schemes and projects he returned to benefit his own dear country, but had the misfortune to find them rejected by the envious ministers of Queen Anne, and himself sent treacherously away.

And hence it is that in his fourth voyage he discovers a vein of melancholy proceeding almost to a disgust of his species; but, above all, a mortal detestation to the whole flagitious race of ministers, and a final resolution not to give in any memorial to the Secretary of State, in order to subject the lands he discovered to the Crown of Great Britain.

Now if, by these hints, the reader can help himself to a further discovery of the nature and contents of these travels, he is welcome to as much light as they afford him; I am obliged by all the ties of honour not to speak more openly.

But if any man shall ever see such very extraordinary voyages into such very extraordinary nations, which manifest the most distinguishing marks of a philosopher, a politician and a legislator, and can imagine them to belong to a surgeon of a ship or a captain of a merchant-man, let him remain in his ignorance.

And whoever he be that shall further observe, in every page of such a book, that cordial love of mankind, that inviolable regard to truth, that passion for his dear country, and that particular attachment to the excellent princess Queen Anne; surely that man deserves to be pitied if, by all those visible signs and characters, he cannot distinguish and acknowledge the great Scriblerus.

CHAPTER XVII

Of the discoveries and works of the great Scriblerus, made and to be made, written and to be written, known and unknown

And here it seems but natural to lament the unfortunate end of the amour of our philosopher. But the historian of these memoirs on the contrary cries out, 'Happy, thrice happy day, which dissolved the marriage of the great Scriblerus! Let it be celebrated in every language, learned and unlearned! Let the Latin, the Greek, the Arabian, the Coptic, let all the tongues of many-languaged men, nay, of animals, be employed to resound it! Since to this we owe such immense discoveries, not only of oceans, continents, islands, with all their inhabitants, minute, gigantic, mortal and immortal, but those yet more enlarged and astonishing views of worlds philosophical, physical, moral, intelligible and unintelligible!'

Here therefore, at this great period, we end our first book. And here, O reader, we entreat thee utterly to forget all thou hast hitherto read, and to cast thy eyes only forward, to that boundless field the next shall open unto thee; the fruits of which (if thine, or our sins do not prevent) are to spread and multiply over this our work, and over all the face of the Earth.

In the meantime, know what thou owest, and what thou yet mayst owe, to this excellent person, this prodigy of our age, who may well be called the philosopher of ultimate causes, since by a sagacity peculiar to himself he hath discovered effects in their very cause, and without the trivial helps of experiments or observations, hath been the inventor of most of the modern systems and hypotheses.

He hath enriched mathematics with many precise and geometrical quadratures of the circle. He first discovered the cause of gravity and the intestine motion of fluids. To him we owe all the observations on the parallax of the Pole Star, and all the new theories of the Deluge. He it was that first taught the right use sometimes of the *fuga vacui*, and sometimes of the *materia subtilis*, in resolving the grand phenomena of nature. He it was that first found out the palpability of colours, and by the delicacy of his touch could distinguish the different vibrations of the heterogeneous rays of light. His were the projects of *perpetuum mobile*, flying engines and pacing saddles; the method of discovering the longitude by bomb-vessels, and of increasing the trade-wind by vast plantations of reeds and sedges.[37] I shall mention only a few of his philosophical and mathematical works:

1. A complete digest of the laws of nature, with a review of those that are obsolete or repealed, and of those that are ready to be renewed and put in force.
2. A mechanical explication of the formation of the universe, according to the Epicurean hypothesis.
3. An investigation of the quantity of real matter in the universe, with the proportion of the specific gravity of solid matter to that of fluid.
4. Microscopical observations of the figure and bulk of the constituent parts of all fluids. A calculation of the proportion in which the fluids of the Earth decrease, and of the period in which they will be totally exhausted.
5. A computation of the duration of the sun, and how long it will last before it be burned out.
6. A method to apply the force arising from the immense velocity of light to mechanical purposes.
7. An answer to the question of a curious gentleman. How long a new star was lighted up before its appearance to

the inhabitants of our earth? To which is subjoined a calculation: how much the inhabitants of the moon eat for supper, considering that they pass a night equal to fifteen of our natural days.

8. A demonstration of the natural dominion of the inhabitants of the Earth over those of the moon, if ever an intercourse should be opened between them. With a proposal of a partition treaty among the earthly potentates in case of such discovery.

9. Tide tables for a comet that is to approximate towards the Earth.

10. The number of the inhabitants of London determined by the reports of the gold-finders[38] and the tonnage of their carriages; with allowance for the extraordinary quantity of the *ingesta* and *egesta* of the people of England, and a deduction of what is left under dead walls and dry ditches.

It will from hence be evident how much all his studies were directed to the universal benefit of mankind. Numerous have been his projects to this end, of which two alone will be sufficient to show the amazing grandeur of his genius. The first was a proposal, by a general contribution of all princes, to pierce the first crust or nucleus of this our Earth, quite through, to the next concentrical sphere. The advantage he proposed from it was to find the parallax of the fixed stars, but chiefly to refute Sir Isaac Newton's theory of gravity, and Mr Halley's of the variations. The second was to build two poles to the meridian, with immense lighthouses on the top of them, to supply the defect of nature and to make the longitude as easy to be calculated as the latitude. Both these he could not but think very practicable by the power of all the potentates of the world.

May we presume after these to mention how he descended from the sublime to the beneficial parts of knowledge, and particularly his extraordinary practice of physic. From the age, complexion or weight of the person given, he contrived to prescribe at a distance as well as at a patient's bedside. He taught the way to many modern physicians to cure their patients by intuition, and to others to cure without looking on them at all. He projected a *menstruum*[39] to dissolve the stone, made of Dr Woodward's universal deluge water. His also was the device to relieve consumptive or asthmatic persons by bringing fresh air out of the country to town by pipes of the nature of the recipients of air pumps; and to introduce the native air of a man's country into any other in which he should travel, with a seasonable intromission of such steams as were most familiar to him, to the inexpressible comfort of many Scotchmen, Laplanders, and white bears. In physiognomy, his penetration is such that, from the picture only of any person, he can write his life; and from the features of the parents draw the portrait of any child that is to be born.

Nor hath he been so enrapt in these studies as to neglect the polite arts of painting, architecture, music, poetry, etc. It was he that gave the first hint to our modern painters to improve the likeness of their portraits by the use of such colours as would faithfully and constantly accompany the life, not only in its present state, but in all its alterations, decays, age, and death itself. In architecture, he builds not with so much regard to present symmetry or conveniency as with a thought well worthy a true lover of antiquity, to wit, the noble effect the building will have to posterity, when it shall fall and become a ruin. As to music, I think Heidegger has not the face to deny that he has been much beholden to his scores. In poetry, he hath appeared under a hundred different names, of which we may one day give a catalogue. In politics, his writings are of a peculiar cast, for the most part ironical, and the drift of them often so delicate and refined as to be mistaken by the vulgar. He once went so far as to write a persuasive to people to eat their own children[40], which was so little understood as to be taken in ill part. He has often written against liberty in the name of Freeman and Algernon Sydney, in vindication of the measures of Spain under that of Raleigh, and in praise of corruption under those of Cato and Publicola.

It is true that at his last departure from England, in the reign of Queen Anne, apprehending lest any of these might be perverted to the scandal of the weak or encouragement of the flagitious, he cast them all, without mercy, into a bog-house near St James's. Some however have been with great diligence recovered, and fished up with a hook and line by the ministerial writers, which make at present the great ornaments of their works.

Whatever he judged beneficial to mankind, he constantly communicated (not only during his stay among us, but ever since his absence) by some method or other in which ostentation had no part. With what incredible modesty he concealed himself is known to numbers of those to whom he addressed sometimes epistles, sometimes hints, sometimes whole treatises, advices to friends, projects to First Ministers, letters to Members of Parliament, accounts to the Royal Society, and innumerable others.

All these will be vindicated to the true author in the course of these memoirs. I may venture to say they cannot be unacceptable to any but to those who will appear too much concerned as plagiaries to be admitted as judges. Wherefore we warn the public to take particular notice of all such as manifest any indecent passion at the appearance of this work as persons most certainly involved in the guilt.

NOTES

1. *Little Book*, or the *Memoirs of Martinus Scriblerus*.

2. warmed by another sun: Horace, *Odes*.

3. The birthplace of the illustrious philosopher, Martinus Scriblerus.

4. Quarles and Withers were two seventeenth-century poets who wrote verse that made a wing pattern on the page. Figure poetry of this kind was later scorned.

5. Jacob Behmen (1575–1624) was a mystic.

6. with raised ears.

7. This chapter satirises Dr John Woodward, a distinguished contemporary scientist and antiquarian, whose claim that his old, embossed shield was antiquarian, was much derided.

8. The *triclinium* refers to beds that surrounded the Roman dining-room table; *decubitus* refers to reclining at the table.

9. *Melchior* was a common name among German theologians in the sixteenth/seventeenth centuries; *insipidus* means stupid.

10. The *cuspis* refers to the point of the sword; *insignia virilia* to the male member; *dii termini* to Terminus, the Roman god, statues of whom marked boundaries; *non bene relicta parmula* misquotes Horace, 'I shamefully throw away my shield'.

11. In this chapter, Pope and Arbuthnot ridicule ancient and modern ideas about how diet forms individual and national character.

12. Games mentioned here include: 'cross and pile' or heads and tails; 'ducks and drakes' or skimming stones over water; 'handy-dandy', a guessing game in which an object is concealed in the hands; 'cinque' or 'mourre', a game in which one player guesses the number of fingers held up simultaneously by another player; 'hot-cockles', a game where a blindfolded player guesses which of the other players has struck him/her.

13. A violent military dance performed in costume.

14. Running.

15. A hall with seats used for debate by philosophers and rhetoricians.

16. to enchant the afflicted places.

17. Nickers was a contemporary word for youths who broke windows by throwing coins.

18. This chapter employs a series of Latin terms to satirise the jargon of philosophers' rhetoric and the empty verbiage employed by logicians and schoolmasters.

19. With its focus on Crambe, this chapter is given over to wordplay and punning, an extremely popular pursuit in the early eighteenth century.

20. Richard Bentley, a scholar, and Francis Hare, a Whig pamphleteer, were both mocked as enemies of the Scriblerus Club.

21. The word 'flux' was applied to the contemporary treatment of syphilis with mercury.

22. It's clearly a desperate case!

23. The pineal gland, where Descartes located the soul.

24. A roasting jack was a machine for turning the spit when roasting meat.

25. Chapters XIV and XV burlesque the plots of contemporary romantic novels.

26. Monomotapa is a region in South Africa.

27. Depending on the source, either India, Ethiopia or Mongolia.

28. Scriblerus marries disreputably, in a debtors' prison.

29. pending the outcome of the case.

30. as from a parent, hereditarily.

31. Plastic here means shaping, reproductive.

32. In Scholastic terminology, the *suppositum* is that which underlies all the accidents of a thing, i.e. the individual substance of a certain kind which is the subject of existence and all accidental modifications which constitute the individual.

33. the generation of one is the corruption of the other.

34. The *ius petendi et reddendi debitum conjugale* is the right of seeking and of rendering the marital duty; *debitum reddendi, nemo tenetur ad impossibile* means as to the yielding, no one is held to the impossible.

35. Martinus' *Travels* are in fact those of Lemuel Gulliver in Swift's *Gulliver's Travels* (1726).

36. *The Case of Straddling and Stiles* is a 1716 satire of legal jargon written by Pope.

37. The *fuga vacui* is the abhorrence of a vacuum; *materia subtilis* is subtle matter; and *perpetuum mobile*, perpetual motion.

38. sewage collectors.

39. solvent.

40. This persuasive is a reference to Jonathan Swift's *A Modest Proposal* (1729).

BIOGRAPHICAL NOTE

Alexander Pope was born in London in 1688, the son of Alexander senior, a cloth merchant, and Editha, both staunch Catholics. Due to the intensity of anti-Catholic sentiment at the time, the family were obliged to move from London when Pope was still young. Pope's Catholic upbringing also had severe implications on his education, and he was forced to study from home, learning Latin and Greek from a local priest, but largely being self-taught.

As a child he suffered from ill health – what is now believed to be tuberculosis of the bone – which severely stunted his growth and led to a lifetime of medical complaints. Sir Joshua Reynolds, in fact, once notoriously described him as 'about four feet six high; very humpbacked and deformed'. Pope began writing from an early age but it was not until the publication of *An Essay on Criticism* in 1711 that he received recognition. As his reputation grew, few could doubt his mastery of poetry – indeed his skill in the heroic couplet and the burlesque were unparalleled, and *The Rape of the Lock* universally regarded as a work of genius. It was as a member of the Scriblerus Club, alongside Jonathan Swift, Thomas Parnell, John Gay and John Arbuthnot, that Pope gave full vent to his attack on intellectual poverty. In collaborative works such as *Scriblerus*, he developed the notion that he first elaborated in *An Essay on Criticism* that 'a little learning is a dangerous thing'.

In later life, Pope developed an interest in horticulture and landscape gardening – passions he pursued from his home in Twickenham. He remained there until his death in 1744, by which time he was regarded as the leading poet and satirist of his day.

HESPERUS PRESS – 100 PAGES

Hesperus Press, as suggested by the Latin motto, is committed to bringing near what is far – far both in space and time. Works written by the greatest authors, and unjustly neglected or simply little known in the English-speaking world, are made accessible through new translations and a completely fresh editorial approach. Through these short classic works, each little more than 100 pages in length, the reader will be introduced to the greatest writers from all times and all cultures.

For more information on Hesperus Press, please visit our website:
www.hesperuspress.com

To place an order, please contact:
Grantham Book Services, Isaac Newton Way
Alma Park Industrial Estate
Grantham, Lincolnshire NG31 9SD
Tel: +44 (0) 1476 541080 Fax: +44 (0) 1476 541061
Email: orders@gbs.tbs-ltd.co.uk

SELECTED TITLES FROM HESPERUS PRESS

Gustave Flaubert *Memoirs of a Madman*
Ugo Foscolo *Last Letters of Jacopo Ortis*
Anton Chekhov *The Story of a Nobody*
Joseph von Eichendorff *Life of a Good-for-nothing*
Mark Twain *The Diary of Adam and Eve*
Giovanni Boccaccio *Life of Dante*
Victor Hugo *The Last Day of a Condemned Man*
Joseph Conrad *Heart of Darkness*
Edgar Allan Poe *Eureka*
Emile Zola *For a Night of Love*
Daniel Defoe *The King of Pirates*
Giacomo Leopardi *Thoughts*

Nikolai Gogol *The Squabble*
Franz Kafka *Metamorphosis*
Herman Melville *The Enchanted Isles*
Leonardo da Vinci *Prophecies*
Charles Baudelaire *On Wine and Hashish*
William Makepeace Thackeray *Rebecca and Rowena*
Wilkie Collins *Who Killed Zebedee?*
Théophile Gautier *The Jinx*
Charles Dickens *The Haunted House*
Luigi Pirandello *Loveless Love*
Fyodor Dostoevsky *Poor People*
E.T.A. Hoffmann *Mademoiselle de Scudéri*
Francesco Petrarch *My Secret Book*
D.H. Lawrence *The Fox*
Percy Bysshe Shelley *Zastrozzi*